WRITING *in* CIRCLES
A CELEBRATION OF WOMEN'S WRITING

A COMPANION TO *WOMEN, WRITING, AND SOUL-MAKING*
BY PEGGY TABOR MILLIN

EDITOR
Peggy Tabor Millin

CO-EDITORS:
Kathleen Rada Boswell
Jennifer Lynn Browning
Deborah Cantrell
Betsy Fletcher
Mary Freen
Vickie Manz
Alicia Porterfiel

D1715202

SUNBURST
CABIN
PRESS

Sunburst Cabin Press
709 N. Rio Vista Blvd.
Fort Lauderdale, Florida 33301
www.clarityworksonline.com

ISBN 978-0-9906891-0-2
Library of Congress Control Number: 2015932760

Cover and interior design by Ginger Graziano — www.gingergraziano.com

Cover photos:
Hands: ©Nvnkarthik/Dreamstime
Zen circle: ©Cienpies Design/Shutterstock

THE ENSO

Zen teachers like to draw circles. Sometimes they draw them around from right to left, sometimes around from left to right. These circles can represent emptiness, fullness, or the moon. Or they can represent the practice. The circle that goes around from right to left—against the path of the sun on the sundial—represents the hard way of practice before any glimmer of understanding appears. When it goes around from left to right, following the path of the sun, it represents the easier way of practice after a glimmer opens the Way. But both before and after the glimmer, the practice requires investment and conscientious diligence.

Robert Aiken, American Zen Master, as quoted in
Enso: Zen Circles of Enlightenment by Audrey Yoshiko Seo

Aiken's description of the enso also describes both the process of Centered Writing Practice, the body-centered, freewriting approach used in writing the works in this book, and the function of the circle in which the women sit to write.

The process of writing practice may be difficult or easier, depending on one's approach. If viewed as a step toward "real writing," as in creating a product, the writer will be aware of trying, laboring over, or pushing toward. When the illumination comes that writing practice is the "real writing," the ground from which all writing springs, then writing becomes easier. Still, all writing requires "investment and conscientious diligence."

Writing in circles, both physical and metaphorical, is the process of "soul-making," through which we expose and release layer after layer of ourselves, circling closer and closer to our true selves, our soul. Symbolically, the circle is feminine, representing the moon with its cycles. The safety of the circle allows us to let go of the outcome and focus solely on the process. As obstacles drop away and healing occurs, our truth emerges.

PTM

DEDICATION

To the circles of women word weavers
spanning our globe

and

To our sisters anywhere whose truths go unspoken
because of discrimination, oppression, and poverty

TABLE OF CONTENTS

A Note from the Editors

On a crisp fall day, seven of us sat chatting in the lodge at Lake Logan Episcopal Conference Center. We had experienced another day of fierce and fearless writing at a seven-day retreat led by Peggy Tabor Millin through her ClarityWorks writing program. From our exchange, an idea was born—a compilation of some of the writing created using Peggy's Centered Writing Practice at the ten years of retreats given at conference centers at Lake Logan and Seabrook and a private home in Montreat.

The ClarityWorks circle of women writers is large and has writers from all over the world, Africa to Albuquerque and points between. Our first task, then, was to narrow our focus so that we could get a manageable number of submissions. We decided that one way to accomplish this goal was to limit our pool of potential submissions to pieces completed by past retreat participants. Doing so gave us a starting point for a project which we hope will grow in the years to come with future volumes that contain work from other ClarityWorks participants, from classes, Peggy's online writing prompts, etc.

The second thing we decided early in our discussion was that, as much as we wanted this work to be a repository for the many wonderful pieces of writing we heard in circle, we also wanted the volume to be a gift to the woman who has inspired each of us to embrace our writer selves. Peggy's guidance has made an impact on the life of each woman who has had the gift of attending one of her retreats or classes. One of our editors, Alicia Porterfield, expresses it this way:

> There's something about writing in a circle of women.
> Peggy provides the parameters for the group, preparing
> the process and providing the prompts and the time
> frame. She primes the pump. Then, when with her simple

"Begin," the pens start scratching on clean, fresh pages, the candle flickers and . . . magic happens. Imaginations spill over onto pages and stories start telling themselves on the page, images fresh or long-buried pop up, nestling themselves wherever they deem best, words link up that never had even been introduced to each other before now, but somehow become the best of friends right there on the page. Before we know it, "time" is called and reluctantly, we let our pens rest. They've been playing hard and so have we, like children coming in from recess, faces still flushed from the sun and wind, eyes bright with all the make-believe that just came true, right there on our pages.

We wanted in some small way to show our gratitude to the woman who can bring such magic to each of us. To that end, we decided that any profit made by this publication would go directly to ClarityWorks.

In this collection, you will find observations, creative non-fiction, fiction, and poetry created by women who have attended retreats at Lake Logan or Seabrook. The topics covered in these selections are varied, yet they also point to the universal experience. Some of the selections are raw and come straight from the circle. Other pieces have been revised and reworked into more polished drafts. Some pieces have even been previously published. We hope that you enjoy reading each of these pieces as much we did.

The Editors

The Offering

Peggy Tabor Millin

Staring into space,
I imagine my destiny, the gift of my life:
A long line of women in bright striped shawls
wend their way up a mountain;
they laugh and cry,
they sing old songs, hold hands.
Each carries a basket of words.
They approach where I stand by an altar—
One by one, each sprinkles her words
like petals across the crystal table,
and says,
These are my words
All of myself
I give to Lord Mother
From whom they came.
The words turn into diamonds,
the diamonds into water, and
the water into rivers
rushing down mountains to nourish the earth.
The women turn into trees and flowers and plants
to hold the Earth together with their roots.
They sing in the wind—of truth, peace,
and all things warm and growing.

Author's Note: Written at Lake Logan 2008 to the prompt "staring into space"

INTRODUCTION
Peggy Tabor Millin

In my lap, sheaves of paper holding the words now inside this
book; beside me on the floor, a Cherokee double-weave basket
made by woman's hands. I think of the poem I wrote six years
ago—women with baskets of words. How the poem fell off my pen
like a walnut from its limb, sure and whole. I pick up the basket,
fingering its textures, following the reeds in and out.

Every spring a woman and her husband drive eighty miles to
gather river cane, cut it with a bush knife and pile it in the bed of
an old pickup. Back home, she scrapes the cane with a hunting
knife and splits each stalk into four long strips with a pocket knife.
Preparing the cane is a three-knife job: it takes over a hundred
strips to weave a single basket.

She has already soaked bloodroot and butternut bark in the old
washtub and made the dyes on a fire in the yard, close enough to
watch her grandchildren play like monkeys in the butternut tree
while she works in its shade. Nearby, five hounds sleep in dappled
sun, jumbled together like a pile of old clothes.

She spirals the cleaned and shaven cane into the dye, moving
from pot to pot, stirring with large sticks bearing the patina of the
hands of her mother and mother's mother. All this toil of gathering,
cleaning, shaving, stirring and she has not yet begun to weave this
small basket that is really two, not yet formed the square bottom that
transforms into a circle at the top. When wet, this basket will hold
water—or repel it. Such a basket must have whisked Moses down
the river to his destiny, much like I feel I was whisked to mine.

I sit in a circle of women writing, feeling satisfied, each of us a reed
offering ourselves to be woven, entwined and then again offering
ourselves to be immersed in the water of the spirit to breathe it in,

to fill ourselves full, and then to exhale until we know what to hold and what to leave out. I love this basket of women, how easily we slide in and out of togetherness, in and out of this community we never quite leave, that holds us with words even when we've gone.

Each time I read "The Offering" aloud in a circle, I cry. I cry for the opportunity I have had to fulfill this destiny of providing an altar on which women can feel free to offer the truth of their hearts through words. I cry for the gift of their trust and love and honor.

In 2011, again at Lake Logan, I wrote this to the prompt "the thing to remember."

"You are not alone," my friend says, and takes my hand. "Look! That's no eagle on the beach, but the eagle within you." She laughs, delighted.

My friend is not a boat taking me on a journey or a beacon shining her light into my heart. She is a mirror in which I see the light radiating from within me.

This is our task, the only task here in what we call the world: to hold the mirror so whoever looks sees her own radiant Self reflected.

The alchemy that occurs in the writing circle allows the women to send down roots deep into their souls and to recognize, however fleetingly, their true identity.

Many women have said to me, "You saved my life."

To one I answered, "Maybe, but you walked through the door."

"Yes," she replied, "but you opened it."

When someone compliments your writing, I teach, you must say with passion, "I accept!" and raise your hands up to the sky. So I also must accept that I open the door for women to claim their voice through writing. I had no idea this was what I was doing when I began. Centered Writing Practice evolved as a defined process while I observed.

From the circle, I learned the double-weave: teacher and student together create a container for the stories each person shares.

The tightness of the weave determines the safety of the group as a whole. Safety allows us to take the risks necessary to write freely, and therefore honestly, from our hearts. No matter what we write, we write ourselves, and this writing heals us—and others—without effort or analysis.

This book is proof of the process's ability to plant creativity and flower confidence. Its contents illustrate the wisdom of Rabih Alameddine who wrote in *The Hakawati*: "*What happens is of little significance compared with the stories we tell ourselves about what happens. Events matter little, only stories of events affect us.*"

I invite you to delve into the stories held in these pages. You will find them poignant, funny, quirky, wise, and sad. They will affect you because they touch commonalities in the experience of women. In reading them, you will see yourself, your own life, reflected. I hope you will take the time to contemplate the courage it takes for any woman to write her truth and to offer her words to others. And, I hope these words inspire you to pick up the pen and write. No matter the topic, the genre, the form, the world needs your story, and only you can tell it.

"I write entirely to find out what I'm thinking, what I'm looking at, what I see and what it means. What I want and what I fear."
Joan Didion

RETREATING INTO WRITING

In the safety of circles,
we learn to respect silence, create safety,
build trust, set boundaries,
resolve conflict, and laugh—
at ourselves and at the vagaries of life.

PTM

There Are a Few Things to Know Before We Start

Amy Slothower

1. Once we start, there is no stopping.
2. You will feel stupid.
3. You will think that you have nothing to say.
4. You may, in fact, have nothing to say.
5. This does not matter; you will write anyway.
6. Sometimes you will write for a very long time.
7. Sometimes you will write for no time at all.
8. The amount you have to say will be inversely proportional to the amount of time given.
9. You will marvel at how quickly, quietly, and confidently those around you can write.
10. Your hand will get cramps.
11. At some point you will stop writing. This is when the fun begins.
12. You will have to read what you have written aloud.
13. Reading aloud is likely to make you do one of three things: blush, cry or laugh. You will hope that the audience has the same, not the opposite, reaction as you have to your own material. You will especially hope that they do not laugh if you cry.
14. You will also get to hear what others have written. This will leave you stunned, awed, amazed, amused, touched, tickled, angry, hysterical, sad, sympathetic, jealous, curious, intrigued, entranced, and enthralled.
15. There will be words of encouragement. These are not like Little-League-everyone-gets-a-trophy words of encouragement. They are sincere and considered and make you want to keep going.
16. In addition to the hand cramps your butt will go numb. And sometimes your forearm and occasionally a foot.

17. After these sessions of shared time, there will be silence. Hours and hours of silence.

18. If you are not writing during these hours of silence, you will feel guilty, even though you have been instructed not to feel guilty. You will have been told that napping and hiking count as writing, but somehow those activities do not fill the lines on the page.

19. Sometimes, the silence will lead to bursts of productivity. During these moments you will think, "I AM a writer. I was meant to do this. I am a genius!" You will be wrong about the genius part.

20. All of this writing will be punctuated with frequent trips to the dining hall. If you take the longer path the walk is half of a mile. You will start doing calculations in your head about how many calories you are burning and whether it will compensate for the gravy-soaked biscuits and cookies with every meal. It will not.

21. As the days pass, you will come to know your fellow writers in a strange way. You will hear some of their most intimate secrets but must pretend those secrets are just fiction. You will see them without their cloaks of make-up and fancy clothes and will wonder what they look like "on the outside." And you will feel connected to them because they understand, when so many others cannot, this odd writing affliction that has plagued you for your whole life. And you will know that they will hold a permanent place in your heart. And you will consider the possibility that perhaps, one day, a few of them may show up as well-disguised characters in a story that you have yet to write.

The (My) Writing Life

Candy Maier

The first afternoon at my women's writers retreat at Lake Logan in Western North Carolina is set aside for free writing time. I am excited about the rare opportunity to have three uninterrupted hours of time to work on a story.

I find the perfect place to write — a small dock jutting out into the crystal blue lake. So beautiful, I know I'll be here all afternoon. I change into my shorts but keep my sweatshirt on for warmth. I pull my baseball cap low over my eyes, since sunglasses alone won't be able to handle the myriad of reflections coming off the sparkling lake. It takes me two trips from the cottage to carry my supplies down to the water's edge — two lawn chairs, one to sit on and one to prop my feet on; my notebook and pen; a blanket; a half-gallon of diet Coke; and two apples. Finally, when I'm all set up, I gaze out at the lake, the trees and the swiftly moving white clouds.

I eat an apple while letting my mind wander, knowing it will settle on the perfect first line of my story. I pull out the Saturday *New York Times* crossword puzzle and fill in some words. After a few minutes, I open my notebook. The wind picks up and it's hard to concentrate thinking that my hat is going to blow off my head. I decide to move up to the deck of the cottage. It takes two more trips to get everything back to the house.

I'm settled again in a rocking chair facing the lake, trying to think of a story idea. Someone in group this morning wrote about a cape. I write about my old boyfriend Harold wearing that stupid cape and wide-brimmed hat the night I broke up with him. He looked more like a pimp than an investment banker, which made it easier to say goodbye. The story goes nowhere and bores me.

I try making a list like our teacher suggests when we are stuck for ideas. I list some of the things my father burned in the fireplace when I was little: the chess set, my mom's Bible, dinner plates, and the chopped up piano. It goes nowhere; I've written too much on that subject already. After a few more false starts, I decide to go to my room to work on the crossword puzzle and take a nap. I doze for twenty minutes. Now it's 3:30 p.m., only one and a half more hours to kill till I can hang out with people.

I stare at the ceiling, getting madder by the minute, listening to the voice in my head. This is stupid. What are you doing here on this retreat? You can't write. You don't even like writing. If tomorrow's free write was in the morning instead of the afternoon, I'd go home early. What the hell am I supposed to do all morning without the Sunday paper? I'm really glad I brought my crocheting.

I decide to go for a walk.

I head out the three-mile-loop trail and after about half a mile see a small cemetery. I'm not surprised, since I've been obsessed with death and dying for the last seven years. Standing in front of a grave, I feel a strong urge to write. I hike back down to the cottage and get my notebook and pen and return to the cemetery and look for a place to sit. The grave of Lucille Rogers Revis sports a tombstone large enough for a comfortable backrest. Before sitting, I read the plaque at the foot of her grave.

If tears could build a stairway and memories a lane,
I'd walk right up to heaven and bring you back again.
We love you Mama.

I'm surprised her children would consider messing with God's will. If they had tried to bring her back from heaven, old Lucille's ghost would probably still be hanging around here waiting to tell them off. After all, heaven might have been the first time in her life she'd gotten to rest and then her kids insist she come back just so they can feel good.

I no sooner write these lines than the wind picks up and howls around me.

"Relax Lucille," I call into the wind. "I just want to sit here a minute and write about wishing I was six feet under like you."

The story to write has found me at last. I pick up my pen.

The Process

When we combine physical centeredness
in the belly and freewriting to neutral prompts
with active practice, both solitary and
in community, we have the
choreography for Centered Writing Practice....
We center in our bellies and put the pen
to paper. No crossing out or lingering over
perfect phrases or searching for metaphors.
Following the pen,
we outrace the conscious mind.

PTM

. . . .

There's Something to be Said

Kathleen Rada Boswell

There's something to be said for the candle that is lit
       every morning
The candle means we are all coming together in our circle
The candle is the muse of our magic
Its steady flame urges us to create
It watches us laugh and cry
It must be lit—it must be there
The candle is the "play" button
Play with your pen on the paper
Play with the words and the sentences
Let your soul play in its light
It is the beginning and the end
There is something to be said about the candle

The Room Disappears into the Present

Kimberly Smith

Eyes turned inward, breath expands.
Far away sounds come near.
The slosh of blood
Echoes in the ears.
The room disappears.
The sounds all recede.
Emptiness for a split second.

Then I notice the emptiness
And it is empty no longer.
The chair returns
Holding my back and backside.
The breath again exchanges
Oxygen and other gases.
The gurgle of a stomach.
The spray of saliva.
My feet are cold.
My ear itches.
That hitch in my back is hitched up again.
I forget what I'm doing here.

And then I remember.
I feel my breath move.
I notice the crow.
I soften and sigh.
I sink again into waiting,
The stillness
…slowly…emerging.
Nowhere to go,

Nothing to do.
I watch mind, no longer mine.
And it's gone.
Disappearing.
Opening to blankness.
That split second that
I watch for.
The second between
The first and the third.
First, second and third
Disappearing into all.
Then everything becomes nothing.

Then the next thought
Reminds me that I'm here.
I'm thinking, therefore I am.
I'm not thinking,
Or rather then, just then,
I wasn't thinking,
Therefore I AM.

Island

Vickie Manz

It's the first writing prompt of the day, "island." A time to float the pen across blank pages without thought beyond the mind. A sea of words begins to wash upon the shore moving rhythmically towards release.

Back and forth the pen moves, picking up speed like the ocean waters just before a storm. Will the pen outrace the eager mind swirling with too many thoughts, too many constrictions?

Push it, push it! Build the storm within; allow the words to crash upon the island shores of the writer's heart. Will it be a summer storm or a full-blown tsunami? Only the pen knows as it laps against the white sand of the empty pages. Each stroke releasing, defining. What will be left? When the last moment of thrust is spent, will the sand be swept clean once again waiting for the next storm?

The mind seeks to stop the flow of words yet the pen grows stronger. Push on mind, your time is limited. The pen like a ranging storm is beginning to reveal some mysterious something that must be released. Push that damn pen; allow its truth to spill upon the shore. Push it, push it....

Fly

Beth Dewan

dragonfly, greenflies, fly away, fly high, eagles fly…Where, where is everyone flying? They are in airplanes, hot air balloons, helicopters, spaceships, kites, hang gliders. Where is everyone going? Why are they trying to get away? They want to float in the air, free from the weight of the world. Sometimes when I am in an airplane and look out the window and can see the horizon and puffs and puffs of cotton-ball clouds, I have an urge to jump and dive into the pure white soft weightless white and feel free. If on top of a mountain and I look down into the beauty of nature and the green carpet of trees, I want to dive into the green sea and wrap my body around the oxygen rich greenness of pure life-living, breathing as they should—unencumbered by the heaviness of life, of living.

The Hag in the Bag

Deborah Cantrell

Good morning, world!
Glad to see me?
It's your own personal, custom-made-just-for-you Hag-in-the-Bag,
Coming to you fresh from crumbling domesticity and marital
turmoil.

I am here to point out all of your flaws, short-comings, and
mistakes.
I am not your friend.
Remember, you don't have any friends.
Who would want to be friends with you, creepy crawler that you are?

My job is to make you miserable!
And, I am very good at it, yes indeedy.

I am living in your inner ear, conveniently close to your equilibrium.
I have invaded your brain circuitry, what little you have.

I remind you constantly of the chaos, clutter, confusion, and
unfinished projects that you, and you-alone-in-the-whole-world,
are responsible for.

I tempt you to blame your husband for screwing up all the time
and making you furious over little things, big things, everything,
and nothing.

I encourage you to feel neglected and unappreciated by your children, deserted by your friends, and ridiculed by perfect strangers.

I advise you to hide and lick your wounds, pull the covers over your head, just "give-up" and pout.

I move around in your head to piss you off, and watch you wallow in misery and self-pity.

I live to make you squirm.
I can make your blood boil, your mind muddle, and your heart break.

Yes, indeedy, I am the Hag-in-the-Bag.

I am the Cat-in-the-Hat…on crack cocaine…only not funny.
I am "Mayhem" dressed in your clothes, frumpy and furious, and living merrily in your brain.

I am the Hag-in-the-Bag.
And, I am sooooo not your friend.

A Writer's Prayer

Lucia Ellis

Dear God,
Hear my prayer.
Hear my deep and most sincere prayer.
My most sincere submission, Lord, is not to a publisher, but to you.
I submit my Work to you. You first.
I submit my Soul to you. You first.
I submit this good day and all that came before, and all that comes after, to you.

Dear Lord, God, King of Kings, Holy of Holies, Infinite Invisible, Higher Power, Inner Voice, One that cannot be held in this good mind,

Guide my pen. Guide my tongue, my thoughts, my prayers and actions, comings and goings, ins and outs, ups and downs, my ideas and intuitions, my desires and fears, my hurts and wants. Guide me, Lord, to do Thy will and Thy will alone.
Take me this day and do with me as you will.

Would you have me Write? Use me as your instrument, as your pen, your pencil, your brush, your stick. Write with me, Lord. I am your instrument.

Would you have me Listen? Hear with me, Lord. Let me hear with your ears. Let me hear Your Voice, Your Still Small Voice thundering loud and louder still in my inner ear. Let me take time on this good day to listen and listen well to Your Voice that ever speaks, ever guides, ever soothes, comforts and inspires.

Breathe me, Lord. Think me. Use me, use me, use me as Your Divine Instrument. Take away my ego—my Easing God Out— that I may be your pure and simple channel.

And Lord, Dear Lord, Dear God,
Please let me Trust.
Trust. Trust. Trust.
That you already know.
That you already know.
That you already know and guide, love and protect, inspire and
use me.

Let me trust, please God,
That you are right here
That you write
And hear
As me
On this good day,
In this Most Sacred Place.

Childhood

Fearlessness applies courage to the task
of exploring our inner selves;
by practicing fearlessness, we learn
not to fear what lies within us...
fearlessness is an invitation
to experience the world
just as it is and just as we are.
PTM

. . . .

Mostly Mattie Moon

Maggie Wynne

This year the family's come apart
like a string of pop beads. Freezing
rain plays hit and run while the tin roof
suggests a nap. I dig into cardboard boxes
on the closet floor. Searching for familiar
faces. Silver fish swim through black
and white stories, sepia portraits. From their midst,
Mattie Moon's face beams. The river
between us becomes a puddle.
I jump.

Her smile says she still knows how
to flirt the fun out of a day. Folks
used to say when Mattie Moon prances
down the road, feet dance to her music.
Life gets happy.

Mattie cleaned our house,
washed and ironed our clothes.
I hung around to listen to the shine
of her whistle and the tapping of her feet.

Don't let a laugh or a song pass you by.
Mattie always said. Life's too good to miss.

It was Mattie who taught me how to whistle
and keep time with my feet. She took pride
in her head-handkerchief, kept her uniform
white and slick as ice, smoothed creases left

when I snuggled close to breathe the warmth
of her scent, her rich world.

Across town someone else tended Mattie's children,
 six of them, until that house fire took
the youngest, Mattie's only girl.
After that, her man took to the bottle.
She lost him too, Momma whispered.

Once at days' end, I heard Mattie cry.
Down in the basement shower, she was singing
a gospel song about a motherless child, a long
way from home. Most mournful sound I ever heard.
Never told Mother, who bragged to her bridge club,
Mattie never missed a day of work.
Now Mother's gone.
I have one empty box and Mattie's likeness in my hand.
Tingle in my lips, itch in my feet, I stand up,
shove the door open against wind and ice.
Whistle down the street.

Ill Wind

Martha McMullen

Snowflakes, tiny like grains of sand, swirl, ascend, plummet. It's the day after Thanksgiving, 1950—too early for snow in New Jersey. The radio booms out news of a surprise blizzard.

Because I am an eighth grader, I hate the idea of becoming housebound with five adults: my family and Larry, sister Betty's soon-to-be fiancé, who is a graduate student at Princeton. I thought Larry cut a handsome figure when he wheeled in on his motorcycle Wednesday afternoon. Betty was excited—she hoped he'd brought a ring.

Mac, my dad, and Mother set preparations in motion for days with everyone in the living room—to manage in the power failure that will surely come. We have done this before. Soon, upholstery fabrics that overlap cover the entrance from the foyer. Mother and Mac gather flashlights, batteries, and candles and organize food. Brother Dan and Larry carry wood inside; Betty and I bring my animals to the warmth. This will be a long storm, maybe several days. At Mac's advice, we all read books. Late morning the power is gone, but Mother has soup hot in the deep-well cooker and has made a pot of coffee, so we are jolly over our camp-out lunch. We feel snug and safe from the outside stormy cold.

Dan suggests a game of Monopoly. We put the board on the floor by the French windows, so we can see without using precious light resources.

"At least it's something to do," says Betty, who has never been fond of games and is not a Monopoly shark like Dan and me.

"I haven't played Monopoly in years," says Larry. "I don't re-member the rules."

Soon we are immersed in the game. Everyone has money and is buying property. Betty folds and returns to her book. Round and round the rest of us go. I can see a showdown coming between Dan and me. We tangle over a house and when I look at my money, I can tell the pile of $500 bills is smaller than it was. I count them. I thought earlier that Larry snitched some bills; now I know for sure.

"Larry, give me back the six $500 bills you took," I say.

"What are you talking about—I didn't touch your money," he replies.

We quarrel a bit, then go on. Dan makes more trouble; money is missing again. This time I do not let go.

Mother pronounces, "That is enough of the Monopoly game—at least for you, Nancy." She makes it sound as if I have done something wrong, but I know better than to protest. I leave the game.

I am tense the rest of the day. Betty and Larry laugh together, but he makes me uneasy. Even if my sister loves Larry, to me he is a rat and a sneak. Mother and Mac are cordial with him. Everyone is fine with him except me—I feel like a person in the discard pile. It's going to be an edgy life for me with Larry as a brother-in-law.

Saturday, snow blows thick then thin. Mac keeps watch and we shovel snow at each letup. The fire keeps the living room warm, and Mother cooks fireplace stew in her Dutch oven. Betty and Larry talk quietly in one corner but have no opportunity to be alone. It is not the weekend any of us envisioned.

Sunday morning, the snow is light, but heavier snow is predicted for later. Betty and Larry go for a walk. He is leaving after midday dinner, as previously planned. Princeton will hold classes tomorrow.

When Betty and Larry return, Betty picks up a snow shovel, and Larry goes inside. In a few minutes, he returns with his bags, which he stows on the motorcycle. "Well, Betz," he says. "I'll be taking off, get going while I can." He straddles the big machine and calls for a kiss. Betty responds with a touch of her lips on his cheek. What's happening? Movie viewing tells me to expect something far more dramatic.

After he turns into the road, I say, "Let me see the ring." Betty does not move. "You are engaged, aren't you?" I ask.

"No," says Betty, "we are not, and he is gone."

"You mean he's gone for now. He'll be back at Christmas, you'll get engaged then?"

"That's what he thinks. He doesn't know it, but I expect to never see him again."

I'm mystified. They've been nice to each other all weekend, kind of snuggly. Whatever happened, happened on the walk. "You mean you're not going to marry him?" I ask.

"Do you think I would marry a man who cheated on my little sister in Monopoly?"

I hug her hard, really hard.

Teaching Moments

Jennifer Wheeling

The large dining room table strained under the weight of the side of elk laid out before several generations of sausage-makers; the youngest member, a precocious nine-year-old boy, skillfully used his knife to cut the meat chunks for the grinder. As the pile of grindable meat grew, the boy commented that, after cutting all of this meat, he was going to be a "Master Meat-Cutter."

His father, eager to impart wisdom, asked, "What does it mean to be a 'master'?"

"It means that you are the best or have the most experience at something."

Agreeing, the father launched into a "teachable moment" that he was sure would go right over the little guy's head.

"When I was a younger man, I worked on a fishing boat in the Pacific Ocean between California and Mexico. We fished for marlin and swordfish, both requiring a very large, sharp hook with a big chunk of bait securely attached in order to lure the big fish in. Only those who had lots of baiting experience were allowed to do that job and were dubbed the 'Master-Baiters' by the crew."

At this point, the adults worked hard to hide their amusement, the dual meaning not lost on their adult sense of humor.

Without skipping a beat, the boy looked admiringly at his father and asked, "Daddy, did you ever earn the right to call yourself a 'Master-Baiter'?"

The father, realizing that he was now in potentially dicey waters, decided that the idea of lying to his child was worse than that of familial humiliation.

"Well, son, it took a lot of practice, but I did earn the title and we caught many, many fish when I did the baiting," he said, now desperate for a conclusion.

Announcing the need for a fresh quarter of elk, the father asked his son to give him a hand. As they exited the room, the fissures in the adults' façade began to crack. When the door slammed, the room erupted in a cacophony of hoots and jeers of laughter. Upon the boy's return, the room's now sober occupants gave nothing away save the glistening trails of mirth's tears still moist upon their cheeks.

Shortly thereafter, the boy's school spring program was announced. The boy was especially passionate to share the life cycle of the trout in his family's ponds, to which his teacher gave him enthusiastic encouragement. The days flew by as he worked diligently on the diagram, and, when it came time for the presentation, he escorted his display proudly.

The auditorium filled with expectant parents, uncontrollable toddlers, and disgruntled teenaged siblings. Presentation after presentation, solo or group, the program proceeded while butterflies abounded in the boy's belly. Then came the sound of his teacher's voice calling his name. It was time!

He shimmied off the bleachers and onto the elevated stage's polished floor, the overhead lights blinding him from locating his family. When his little sister announced their relationship, his chest swelled with pride, the butterflies exiting forthwith.

He sensed that the audience had become lethargic as he launched into his presentation. As if to confirm his notion, a father, in the front row, yawned and slouched in his seat. Throttled, the boy considered why this grown man would not find his information riveting. He determined he was going to have to come up with a fact that would really teach him something.

Quiet settled across the stage as the boy churned through his memory for interesting fish facts, when he came upon his most recent "lesson." Without hesitation, he stretched closer to the microphone, to insure that the front-row father would hear him clearly.

"My father worked on a fishing boat that caught big fish. Because the hook was so sharp, it had to be baited just right. Only the best men were trusted to do this job. Those men earned a special title and my father was the ship's best 'Master-Baiter'."

The boy grinned and nodded, the expression of "betcha didn't know that" focused directly on that front-row father, now bolt upright, his face positively joyous at this incredibly informative piece of education. Radiant in his accomplishment, the boy scanned the audience, noting the same expression on all the adults' faces. Huge satisfaction at having shared something so informative fed his ego.

He noticed that his mother had a similar expression but, wait, where was his father? He saw the familiar short-cropped hair of his father's head bent low; that, he deduced, meant that his little sister had lost something under her seat. Finally, when his father's scarlet face appeared, the boy thought it only appropriate to signal the family's sign of a good job, a double thumbs up, before spinning around and marching back to the bleachers.

Grandmaw Effie

Vickie Manz

Leaving the warmth of my mountain retreat, I head out on an early morning walk before breakfast. Enveloped in the stillness, my thoughts roam freely as I slip unexpectedly into a childhood memory of my Grandmaw Effie. This woman who touched the small child in me comes into the present moment, wrapping me in a warm embrace once again.

She reaches out to me now with gnarled hands, worn and used up from a life of hard country living. Her salt and pepper hair, never cut, is pulled neatly into a tight bun at the nape of her neck. Her face lights up with a smile, just for me, revealing teeth, brown from years of brushing snuff absently across them.

Grandmaw Effie loved me best. I knew this by the special look she gave me when our family of six showed up unexpectedly to spend the weekend, as we often did. Grandmaw Effie lived with my Aunt Edna and Uncle Billy in a two-room shack perched on a clay-covered hilltop in Western North Carolina. It was home to her, the one safe place where I always felt loved.

I remember when my Grandmaw Effie went missing. I was a young mother living in Florida, too far away to make a difference. The mountain community where she had spent her entire life was out in force searching for her. They found her tiny body curled up like a small child under a thicket of mountain laurel early on a cold January morning. The mystery of her death was never solved.

I remember cold afternoons when Grandmaw Effie would thrill me with ghost stories as we huddled together on our wooden chairs next to the potbelly stove, our knees inches from the hot metal. Stories of picking apples in the orchard when her mother or Aunt Nora would appear, both long dead. Caught up in the telling, she dipped away at her snuff can with her tiny hickory brush.

The trips to the spring were my favorite. Grandmaw Effie, with a bucket in each hand, would call out to me to come and join her. To reach the spring-fed pond seemed to take forever, yet it was never long enough. Deep in the woods lay a small pond offering the sweetest water I ever tasted. A rough wooden plank lay across the pond allowing Grandmaw to step towards the deeper center where she filled both buckets. She always allowed me time to dip my feet into the icy water and chase butterflies. Our trip back was much slower, the buckets so heavy.

I remember later taking the large water dipper from its nail beside the wooden shelf on the back porch where the buckets of water were kept. I would scoop a full dipper, taste the sweet refreshing coldness of the water and know my Grandmaw would keep those buckets full just as she kept my heart full of her love.

The Wooden Bobbin

Heidi Stewart

A simple wooden bobbin: they don't make wooden bobbins any-more, you know. But I remember Momma's sewing box that my brother made for her in Cub Scouts, full of every color of thread you can imagine, all on wooden bobbins. Momma loved to sew; she would sit at her machine and create all kinds of things, like the quilt she sewed to keep us warm while we traveled all over Europe, riding in the red and white Volkswagen camper. I still remember that it was made with pink flannel and tied with yarn, and we snuggled under its warmth as we reached the top of the moun-tain in the Swiss Alps. She made dresses for me, curtains for the windows and pillows for the window seat in my lavender and lace bedroom, and costumes for my brother's Cub Scout troop's plays.

I learned to sew along with Momma, learned to love the feel of fabric, and now, just like her, I can't go into a store without feeling the fabric as I shop. My stepfather called it a "fabric fetish." What-ever it is, it is an amazing feeling, almost therapeutic, or medita-tive when I go into a fabric store with the intent of picking out a thread, an embroidery floss, a fabric, carefully deciding what thread will go well with the fabric. And then, the feeling of satisfaction and triumph with my choices as the woman at the checkout takes them and cuts the pieces of fabric while saying things like, "what a pretty color," or "I just love this pattern!"

My mother, sewing at her machine, always had a look of sat-isfaction and contentment. A place she could call her own, a place where she could create, a place where she could define and express herself as fully as she wished, a place where she could make a quilt to keep her children warm or something dainty for herself to wear. The sewing box held each shiny spool of thread on an individual bobbin holder made of a wooden dowel. It was covered with contact paper, two sides held together with hinges, and had a latch that closed it with a hook and eye. It also held baby food jars with pins and needles, buttons, and all sorts of sewing machine attachments. I remember sitting on the floor as a child beside her as she worked. I would quietly take the spools off, one by one, stacking them, color coordinating them, using them to make roads for my brother's Matchbox cars, letting my imagination run free.

I sometimes wonder about people who don't know the joys of thread and fabric, who never had the joy of sewing, never knew that thread spools were once wooden, who never had a Momma who would sew and create wondrous things with a simple spool of thread and a piece of fabric and perhaps some lace or rickrack. In the world of sewing, life is simple; it is just the newness of a spool of thread and a piece of fabric from which you can create whatever you wish. Momma knew this, and I can still see her in my mind's eye as she sits and contemplates her next move, her next stitch, as the thread runs up and down and out through the eye of the needle of the Singer sewing machine, her hands gently guiding the fabric along the intended path. Pieces of thread not used lying all over the floor, bits of fabric, her sewing case next to her, made for her with love by her oldest son, all of the children knowing that this was her "throne," her spot, her place to be herself, where she could be alone with her thoughts.

Momma said that she had always wanted a sewing room, where she could leave the machine up and the ironing board out and just close the door on the whole mess and then go back to it whenever she wanted to.

Funny thing, I heard myself say the very same thing the other day as I was working on a quilt, just a spot to call my own, to be by myself, to stack the fabric squares, to be messy, to create and let my imagination run free, and to enjoy just being where I am, the spools of thread beside me.

Who Will She Be?

Joanne Costantino

She has the most disarming little dimpled smile
Green eyes and silky brown hair
Cute as a button, some might say
Pretty, petite, and willful and stubborn
All wrapped up in a pretty little package
Of piss and vinegar, in a frilly white ruffled blouse
That is deceptive, don't be fooled
She will draw you in like a snake in a tree with that little smile
That soon turns into a grin that soon turns into a smirk
That soon turns into a grimace and then it happens,
Todzilla roars to life.
It is a freak of nature that such a tiny being
Can make such a cacophony
There are days when it seems
She has been three for three years
The terrible two's felt like a decade
So that is progress, maybe.
Today she is Todzilla.
With all piss and vinegar and
The willful stubbornness that
Easily runs through her veins and brain
Her power surges are fueled by some unknown source
That needs to be unplugged.
Unplugging that would be wrong.
Her life force will serve her well someday
While it sucks the energy of us all right now.
Today's piss and vinegar is the formula
For tomorrow's bewitching charisma.
She will be special and strong.

This Is Where I Live

Lucia Ellis

I am eleven years old. This is the first time I am having my picture taken.

Mama fixed my hair and I like feeling all the perfect puffy bumps on my head.

Aunt Lula made my dress, and it fit perfectly. It hides everything.

Grandma gave me the earrings.

And he gave me the necklace.

His name is James Gotukola and he is my husband.

Today is our wedding day.

I know I look younger than eleven years, and for all I know, I am. Time-keeping is never accurate in my village.

James Gotukola is Papa's cattleman. James Gotukola sits on the hill most days making sure snakes and hyena don't bother the herd. James Gotukola took my arm one day and laid on top of me. He hurt me. And now he is my husband. If you look carefully at the picture, you will see the little bump that will be my son Edward. Edward Gotukola.

I have seen a lot in my life. These eyes, these good, clear eyes, have seen so much. Someone would say "too much." I do not know.

I have seen Papa hit Mama with the cooking pot. I have seen her lying in the dirt, the yard dog licking blood from her skull. Papa would not let us help her. He stood back and said, "Do not touch her for she is foul and dirty and only worth a yard dog's tongue."

I have seen Mama splash boiling soup in Papa's face. He roared like a lion and we ran outside, afraid of his clawing hands and his bellows.

I have heard the screams and cries of my friends on their special day, the day Mama Kimba cut them with her shard of glass and threw that part to the chickens. I have heard their screams. I have heard my own. There is nothing to do and nowhere to go when strong hands hold your shoulders down and pull your legs apart and cut you. There is nothing to do and nowhere to go, but scream and scream and go inside, deep inside.

This is where I go. Deep inside. To a place where these eyes, these good, clear eyes see only the yellow of the butterfly, and the green grass of the cattle on the hill. These good eyes see only the rich blue of the sky in those few days between rain and dry. This is where I live now. Deep inside.

As I prepare food and clothing for James and Edward Gotukola, this is where I live. Deep, deep inside.

Author's Note: This piece was written to a photo prompt which depicted, presumably, a very young African girl standing next to a seated middle-aged man.

The Quiet Crucible of the Motherless Child

Suzanne Blievernicht

Showering,
her gaze follows the tide
sliding south
to Connection Central
where soapsuds pool
in the eddies of her belly button
caressing the sacred link.

>Tears cascade unabated
>like parched saltines
>crumbling
>searing her lips
>with saline.
>It is her first natal day
>as an orphan,
>>decommissioned.

Destroyers aim compasses west

Cruise ships' horns bellow dirges
in unison
saluting her vessel
that has set sail
through the lifting fog
on San Diego Bay.
Outside her window, two gulls bicker.

>While waves ebb and swell,
>the mountain in motion

in her throat
casts her adrift
gasping,
bereft,
relieved
   of duty.

Family

We do not need to analyze ourselves or dredge up memories or
work on self-improvement. We
only need to be willing to learn
who we are and what the depth
of our soul truly wants and needs
to express. While sharing our
writing in a safe circle, we learn
to trust this process and thereby
trust ourselves.

PTM

. . . .

Perspective

Kathy Sievert

I'm good at this:
standing still and wishing I were somewhere else.
Learned it from my Dad
when I had to hold the flashlight steady
while he bent over the car, hood lifted
open as a cadaver,
exposing the engine
battery and radiator, pumps and coils
cylinders and hoses, belts and dipsticks,
complicated as human anatomy.
He dutifully
tutored as he tinkered.
"Girl's gotta know these things,"
he'd say. "You can't always trust a mechanic."
Mostly I stared at the back of his head,
listened to the laughter of kids playing on the street,
and daydreamed about meeting a boy
who knew how to change a timing belt.
Lately I wonder:
am I still the passive bystander
waiting, watching for the right moment
to shine the light on
unknown highways headed for
the vanishing point?

Watch

Jennifer Wheeling

Watch your thoughts. The phrase that I learned from my mother and that I have taught my girls. How many times have I demonstrated that phrase? Untold numbers. Like in Paris, when the pickpocket stole my wallet on the Metro and I was fearful of the contents of the wallet being lost to identity thieves, I stopped and watched my thoughts, changed their direction and demanded that good was more powerful than evil. The wallet was found, intact, and returned by a kind stranger. Or, when my sister felt the need to tell me that I was not financially supporting our church enough and I got so angry and hurt that she was so bold in her announcement and I didn't watch my thoughts and broke my needed utensil in my anger and have yet to forgive her.

The Plot

Betsy Fletcher

Her parents were getting on in years and she was doing all she could, seeing to their needs. Living as far away as a Georgia girl can get and still reside in the lower forty-eight was challenging. Washington State was the place she currently called home but here she was again, in the land of her birth, doing her duty.

She flew south often, assisting with the cooking so her father could have a few days off from the kitchen. She took her mother to appointments and spot cleaned the kitchen floor in between. Why she was so obsessive about that gold linoleum from the late seventies was as clear as the layered scum of Mop & Glo.

What a metaphor for this family, she thought, *all Mop & Glo on the surface, layer upon layer, year after year.*

"Everything is just fine, fine, fine," they insisted.

In her mind, life, in this moment, was anything but fine.

She wanted to cut through the family surface crap all right, but speaking her mind so freely on any topic was an assault to her parents' Mop & Glo *modus operandi*. She preferred being straight-forward, which directly opposed the rules of the southern social code with which she was raised. Being direct was labeled as "Yankee behavior," according to the code. She felt like a stranger in a strange land. She sighed and thought, *Where was this going? Where are we all going?*

Quite literally, she and her parents would all end up at Shady Grove Cemetery one day. They spoke of the cemetery the previous evening: Shady Grove, where all the ancestral dots were connected for her family, headstones among cedars. She loved that cemetery and her parents loved all the discussion, the details around the end of their lives, the last moments, the funeral arrangements, and being laid in their final resting place on the Mobley plot. Hers and her parents' places were reserved well in advance of departure. She had always imagined lying peacefully underground next to Mema, her paternal grandmother, with her parents close by.

Reviewing the plan for her parents' burial, she was surprised they had come up with a new idea. They now wanted to be planted in the Powell plot with her mother's people, up the hill, not too far. Her parents revealed that the impetus behind the shift in plan had come in order to accommodate her brother and his own Mop & Glo dysfunctional branch of the family.

Her response to the change was as clear as Krud Kutter on the scum of gold linoleum. There was no way she was going to spend eternity with THOSE people on the Mobley plot. Her brother and his family had lived like an island for years, even though they resided only a ninety minute drive away. There was little connection to Shady Grove or the traditions of the past.

What was up with this? she wondered. *Yet, why was she not surprised?* Over and over her parents provided for the brother and his tribe, which was part of the larger family problem. Now it looked like it would be an eternal one.

"Make room for me on the Powell plot," her inner Yankee announced, knowing already that space was limited.

Her mother, sensing the dilemma, spoke up, "Well, we can dig deep and lay stacked instead of side by side, you know, like they do in Europe."

Aging had altered her mother's memory of the density of Georgia clay. It would take a backhoe on steroids to get the three of them properly stacked, layer upon layer like the Mop & Glo floor. Yes, they'd be snapped and sealed, six to eighteen feet under, where "everything was going to be just fine, fine, fine" for the rest of time. She could hardly wait.

Invisible Pink Roses

Mary Freen

Plastic flowers are more practical than real flowers. They last. And last. Maybe that's why people often place them at a grave, small symbols of immortality. But real flowers just seem to hold so much more love. Even the memory of real flowers, not even real—imagined—sometimes those hold the most love of all.

My mother's funeral was a small gathering, just close family around a graveside casket decorated with a huge floral arrangement. My sister had ordered it—the "half-casket cover in delicate pastel shades,"—and she had made a point to request "pink roses, please." It sat there wide and tall, resplendent, but no pink roses, only gaps where roses should have been.

I suppose someone had whisked it off the table before the florist was quite finished. The someone had loaded it in the delivery van, a bit overeager that these flowers not be late for the funeral of a mother dearly loved but gratefully resting and ready to move beyond those final years of senility.

The gaps were glaringly obvious to us, the children of the mother who loved pink roses, but it was a beautiful medley after all. Perhaps it didn't look terribly sparse to anyone else. And what was done was done. It certainly wasn't the biggest disappointment Mom had faced in her ninety-one years. Sad was all I could feel that day, but looking back, I suspect she just laughed about those invisible flowers, as heartfelt a tribute as any real—or plastic—flowers ever were.

When Silence Fell with a Thud

Lucia Ellis

I opened the door…the big…the great big…heavy wooden front door…of 63 Murray Boulevard, home of Rory Goldman and her fancy family—right there on the Battery. I opened the door—must've been around six or seven or eight that Sunday evening—and there stood Mama. Silent.

And I knew. I had already known. I knew the moment she'd called to say they'd be a little late in picking me up. I knew then—that he was gone. That he was dead. I knew, the moment she'd said, "Daddy's not feeling well," that he was dead. Because Daddy never not felt well. Not once in my barely fifteen years had my father, Healer of the Sick, not felt well. So I knew.

I wandered aimlessly around, internally at least, during those long hours between the afternoon phone call and her arrival at their door. I'd been staying over at my friend's house that weekend as Daddy and Mama drove my brother Robert to Atlanta, to Emory, to his first day at college. It was on the way back, between Augusta and Columbia—Mama was driving that leg of the trip—that Daddy said, "Joannie, pull the car over," and she did. And he died—right then and there. Right then and there. On the Spot.

Talk about silence. Talk about Silence falling. Talk about Silence Falling with a Thud.

By the time I opened the Solomons' front door that night, I had already stood under the shower in Rory's bathroom, weeping hard and silent. Praying, "God, God, please don't let him die." But I knew. I knew.

Perhaps it wasn't the first intuition I ever had, but it was certainly the most memorable.

By the time I opened that door and saw my mother's face, nothing had to be said. She shook her head slightly. Even that was unnecessary.

And then, and then…I do not know. I do not remember getting home that night. I do not remember going to bed or waking up the next morning.

I remember standing in the synagogue. September 1968. Feeling not unlike a Kennedy, a Jewish Kennedy. The Kennedys meant funerals to me. I remember the sanctuary, packed with white people; the lawn, packed with black people. That was Charleston in 1968. Probably not so very different now—at least, I wonder. My father was beloved. I was fifteen and bereft and startled and dramatic. I touched the coffin as it passed—as much for effect as for love. Perhaps only for effect. I couldn't salute like John-John, but I could romantically drag my finger along the smooth wood—sorrowful and longing.

The Captain (an excerpt)

Jennifer Browning

May 15, 1884. Elsbet doesn't feel well today. She hasn't come out of her room since Tuesday. The wet nurse and the nanny both assure me that there is nothing to worry about. New mothers, they say, often have such reactions. It's been three months, however, since Daniel Jedidiah was born. We named him after Elsbet's father; William Jedidiah Johnson was one of my favorite men for years. It honored me to name my first-born son after him. I also thought that perhaps doing so would make Elsbet more content with the child. She hardly ever holds our son. When she can be persuaded to join me for an evening in the sitting room, the baby stays safely in his nanny's arms. Elsbet ignores them both unless the baby starts to fuss. Then, focusing on them for a moment, she brusquely commands the nanny to take the boy away. I've tried to talk to her about it. Just last night we had another disagreement. No doubt today's ailment is another of her quiet responses to my disapproval.

Millicent will be here soon to visit for a month or so before going on to Richmond to visit their mother. Elsbet always seems more content when her sister is nearby. Perhaps I should send her back to Richmond with Millicent for a visit. Perhaps that will bring her around.

I just can't understand her reaction to our son. He is perfect in every way. He looks at me with great intelligence whenever I hold him. His blue eyes fix on mine, and I am sure he is only moments from speech. The nanny tells me it will still be several months before he will be able to, but I think she will be proven wrong. My son is so smart. I'm sure he'll have the hang of it much sooner than other babies.

May 15, 1884. Addendum. I have promised elsewhere in this text to be forthright and complete in my observations. I find words hard to compose this evening. My heart is no longer in my chest. I've had to cut it out in order to deal with what has happened. My darling boy is gone. The nanny says he was a bit flushed this morning, but nothing seemed awry. By the time they came to me in the study, his limbs trembled with a fever. I sent for a doctor from town. There had been a bad birthing early in the morning down on the river, and the doctor had not yet returned from there. Our nanny and wet nurse did all they knew. They even tried an old cure of boiled onions piled on his chest. By the time the doctor came, the baby's lips and fingertips were tinted blue. The doctor said we'd done all we could do, but the baby was going to die. I sent for Elsbet. She sent back word that she was still too weak from her headache to leave her bed.

I held my son in my arms as he took his last breath. He looked so intelligently at me right before he closed his eyes. I'm sure he knew how much I wanted him to hold on.

The nanny took him from my arms. She wept silent tears as she started cleaning him and arraying him in fresh clothing.

I had to get out. I had to get away. I came here. I closed the door to my study and left my poor boy in the care of his nanny.

Elsbet remains in her room. I told the housekeeper to let her know that her son is dead. If I had gone to her myself, there would be two caskets prepared for tomorrow.

Waiting for Sam

Joy Wallace Dickinson

Millie wished they didn't have to wait for their brother, but there they were again—just like they were every September—she and her four sisters waiting for Sam to come pick them up to go visit Mama's grave.

It was the only time they got together, the six of them, and it was an uneasy gathering, punctuated by bursts of memory but mostly laced with threads of resentment over slights long forgotten.

None of the others had talked to Margaret in years, for example—except when they had to, like today—and there she was, looking like thunder in calico as she leaned against the wall.

Millie couldn't even remember how that had started: why they didn't talk to Margaret. She would have to ask Little Bert, the sister to whom she was closest, the one who sat beside her now as Millie clutched her handbag, wondering if Sam were really coming.

Maybe he was drunk again—could that even be possible? Bert had told her that Sam had given up whiskey, but he had said that before. Last year when they were ready to leave the cemetery, he was nowhere to be seen. Then Bert found him, passed out and hugging a tombstone.

Bert was well into her sixties, but they still called her "Little Bert" because Mama had been Big Bert. They were all at least sixty, except for Martha, the youngest sister.

Martha was all right, Millie thought. She was the one who had never married and had stayed home to take care of Mama. But the next-to-youngest, Mabel, had gone far away to the Big City and become an artist. She wore big beads and some kind of poncho thing and talked like she was so much better than the rest of them. Once she had even seen Clark Gable on the street—or so she said.

Why in God's name had Mabel come back to this dust bowl

to visit Mama's grave, Millie wondered—why had any of them come after all this time? Maybe they all worried that if they didn't, Mama would know and her ghost would come to get them. Fat lot of good Mabel's fancy poncho thing would do her then.

Millie's fingers tightened on her purse handle. Well, it will be over soon, she thought. There's that no-good Sam now, churning up dust as he makes the turn off the Cimarron Road, driving like a bat out of hell.

Tom

Cindy Peterson

Memories of you as I walk the garden path…

Thursday's sauna night. My kids called it Naked Man Night, seeing the curl of smoke rise from the wood fire in your hand built sauna and you out collecting a bowl full of lettuce from the garden path. The ritual that goes back many years—maybe twenty, maybe thirty. In the early years a few women came. Me too, early on—but the women dropped out, tiring of the long philosophical debates. Tom, the master of sarcasm and slightly inappropriate remarks. But somehow, you became the gathering one. There was a core group of old friends, faithful to the end, who never allowed sauna night to lose its priority. When our kids were small, they would play in the cedar hot tub, the women gathered in the kitchen for a glass of wine and the men would sauna.

It was unusually warm for an early February night. Warm enough for the daphne to bloom. Warm enough to throw the lead-framed window open in the pine-paneled room with the slanting ceiling, allowing a fresh breeze to mingle with the sadness.

"Can I go in?" I asked his oldest son, who stood vigil outside the door. Our eyes met, brimming with sorrow. I knew he was gone, but I wanted to say goodbye one last time to the brother with whom I shared the garden path.

Thirty-three years we had lived side by side, on land home-steaded by my grandparents. Our homes were woven together by my grandmother's garden. Another brother on the other side.

We had learned how to live together, share our lives, share our kids, share our tools and chickens—though we, ourselves, Tom and I were very different. As different as siblings can be, yet there was deep mutual respect and love.

And so many shared stories. So many.

Tom is dead. Choosing not to keep throwing modern miracles at a body weary from the fight.

He said, "No more."

And so we closed our mouths, no more to say.

We knew—all of us knew—he was being true to what he believed. So we stood by and watched the storm of death play out. It only took three days, but it was a violent and brutal storm.

So I came to see him finally at peace—lying still and cold, in his own bed, in his own home. So in my own soul I could rest—knowing the storm was over.

I kissed him on the forehead. Moonlight shown across the bed and up the old wood walls.

Life around here will never be quite the same—

but it will go on and we will remember you.

Your courage. You died as you lived. True to yourself.

The Suit My Brother Never Wore

Kathleen Rada Boswell

For my brother DJ, 1958 – 1998

When my brother was born my father was delighted and so proud to have a son. He purchased a brand new top-of-the-line camera in order to catch all the moments and milestones of the boy who was going to carry on his name. But that was not to be.

He never wore the little suit with a clip-on tie for the first communion picture. He couldn't read or understand the catechism.

He never wore the suit with the tie that my father would have taught him to knot, standing behind him in the mirror, showing him how to measure and cross it over until it was just right. That father-son moment never happened.

My brother never wore the prom suit with the cummerbund to match his date's dress. There was no photo of the boutonniere being pinned to his lapel to record him growing into a man.

He never wore the suit with a crisp starched shirt and perfectly shined shoes for a first job interview.

He would never wear the rented tuxedo, standing nervously at the front of the church waiting for his beautiful bride to appear.

My brother with his big brown eyes and long thick lashes was diagnosed at the age of six as being "borderline retarded." It meant he was just mentally handicapped enough to know he would never keep up with others his age. He knew he would never have a girl-friend or earn enough money to be an independent man. He had a terrible speech impediment that made his words stuttered and thick. He knew people couldn't understand him and would become frustrated to tears trying to repeat his sentences over and over.

He knew there would never be the normal rites of passage for him. He wouldn't ever be the team quarterback or catch a baseball in a well-oiled glove. No Little League team pictures were put on the refrigerator or trophies lined up on a shelf in his room. No learner's permit or official driver's license for him at sixteen. He eventually did learn to drive through my mother's persistence, but only drove to his job as a janitor at a local manufacturing plant. The one time he tried to go somewhere else he got lost and some Good Samaritan called my parents to come get him. He never tried again.

My brother knew that he would not carry on the family name, and he knew that his father wasn't proud of him.

My brother did put on a suit three times in his life. He did so for both his sisters' weddings. In the wedding pictures he stands out as different, but if you didn't know him or our family you wouldn't know why. His face, which in another life would have strongly resembled John Travolta's, was immature. His facial development stopped and rested in the limbo between being a child and being a man. His grin was too big, like a preschooler trying to smile for his class picture.

He lived out the last of his life in our downstairs rec room watching Nick at Night and using a magnifying glass to read the TV guide. No one got him glasses when his eyes began having a hard time reading the small print. Yes, he did learn to read but never beyond a second or third grade level. He sometimes cried for no apparent reason but with great sadness. I wondered if it was because he dreamed of being normal. Did he dream of being perfectly understood? Did he dream of being a man?

He got a blood clot because of complications from a broken ankle that went to his lung at the age of thirty-nine. He was put on a respirator and left to spend the rest of his life with no speech in a hospital bed. He died at age forty because of staph infections that drugs could no longer treat. The doctors made me make the decision to take him off the respirator and watch his breathing stop. He then wore a suit for the third and final time.

I have made peace (kind of) with why my brother's life was so sad. I have to believe that for some reason he chose before he was born to have this life being different than others. I have to believe that his karmic debt is paid. I have to believe that in his next life he will be handsome and happy and participate in all life's events that require a suit. I have to believe.

Kill the Lamp

Kimberly Smith

"Kill the lamp," Johnny whispered.

Clyde reached over and turned the knob on the kerosene lamp.

They held their breaths, listening hard.

"What?" Clyde whispered.

"Hush," Johnny said, finger to his lips. He pointed upward and slowly circled the cabin toward the corner where his rifle leaned. He grimaced as he cocked open the chamber, reached for two shells out of a nearby box, willing the device to be silent. He slowly shut the chamber by placing the barrel under his arm, trying to muffle the sound. He looked up at the ceiling again and tiptoed toward the fireplace, not yet lit for the night.

The December chill was beginning to creep into Clyde's hide and he shuddered. *Johnny's had some bad whiskey again,* he thought. There was absolutely nothing out there and certainly nothing on the roof. He leaned toward a window and slowly pulled aside the curtain for a peek. Nothing to be seen—no moon, no stars, just dark gloom. He looked upwards as far as he could, pressing his cheek into the frosty window pane. Nothing.

Johnny knelt by the fireplace, pushing aside last night's half-burned stump. He leaned into the ashes and peered up the flue. Clyde whispered, "Johnny, there's nothing out there, you crazy coot."

Johnny glanced back and waved his rifle, fingers at the ready. "Of course there is," he hissed. "It's Christmas Eve!"

All Good Things: A Sevenling

Sue Larmon

All good things come in threes:
like dating, marriage, and
the duty of the '60s, parenthood.

All bad things are equally threes:
like alienation, divorce, and
rejection by one's children.

He who pursues the good, must accept the bad.

Author's Note: A sevenling is a poem of seven lines with a mysterious or offbeat tone that invites guesswork from the reader. The first three lines contain three connected or contrasting statements, or a list of three details, names, or possibilities. Lines four to six also contain an element of three, connected directly or indirectly or not at all. The seventh line should act as a narrative summary or punchline. (adapted from Roddy Lumsden)

An Old Book and a Young Friend

Joanne Costantino

I gave an old book to a perfect stranger, though not a total stranger. He's a young man who busses tables at a bayside restaurant in Somers Point, New Jersey. One afternoon while having lunch with friends, he overheard our discussion on television schedules and heard the words "Stephen King." We were discussing the merits of watching *Under the Dome* on television, having not read King's book by the same name.

Apparently, this young man had just finished reading one of the many novels that Stephen King published in the late '70s and again in the '80s with re-written openings. Although the young man politely inserted himself into our conversation, I was genuinely impressed with how effusive he was about Stephen King and just how much he had read and knew about King's early works.

As he went on about this particular novel, I knew he had read one of the later editions of this piece. Being a fan of Stephen King's early works, rather than his later, I offered that he probably had not read the book with what I believed to be the better opening chapter and that the initial opening was far more scary than the re-write he probably read. I was sure the earlier printing was probably published before he was born. When asked where he picked up this particular book, he explained it was a paperback he borrowed from the library. I ask you, how much more charming can this get? A seventeen-year-old kid with a summer job at the Jersey shore who reads library-loaned paperbacks during summer vacation?

As we continued our lunch, I was teased incessantly about being the cougar with a jailbait stalker fan. This young man is the same age as my granddaughter. I found him charming and real without some of the obnoxious lack of common social skills I see in some teens his age. To avoid the appearance of a cougar crush, I'll move on to the point of this little story.

My husband, leader of the teasing campaign, said, "Don't you have the original version of that book at home?" I hesitated, because I doubt he pays that close attention to my book collection(s); he's a big crime-and-lawyer fiction fan who could be president of the James Patterson fan club.

But I responded with the affirmative, mentioning, "Yes, it's the copy I found at a flea market; it has the original dust jacket. It was the best cover of all the printings and the original opening."

Hubby then graciously said, "Let's bring it back for him next time we come in."

While I do collect a relatively odd variety of books—with a personal appreciation I enjoy—I was surprised that my husband remembered something inanimate that has been sitting around for more than twenty years.

The following week, my husband reminded me to pack the book for our young friend. When I found it and dusted it off, I started to thumb through this book slowly, like saying goodbye to an old friend. I double-checked that it was, in fact, the edition I remembered reading back in the late 1970s. With a sigh, I shut it, preparing to send it off to appreciative hands.

We noticed this young man again while at lunch and asked if he would like the book we brought. He was elated, practically blown away. This is no exaggeration. It was a pleasure to make a teenager so happy at the gift of a book, and an old one at that.

I do not mention the title of the book because later in the day someone asked me if I knew if the book had any value as a collectible. I never considered that a book of contemporary popular horror fiction would be worth anything more than the jacket price or less, depending on the condition of the book, so I googled it.

I found that an autographed first edition in pristine condition is worth a considerable amount of money to a collector. This book was in "good" condition, had someone's name written on the inside, not Stephen King's, and I am not a collector of such things.

I want to believe that my "new friend" isn't either. What I do know is that the reaction we enjoyed when I passed this book on to him was very gratifying. He was gracious, openly grateful, and showed off the book to his co-workers, who were interested, pointing to us, as if we had given him a Christmas gift.

The cougar teasing continued later when my husband asked me how I would respond when my young friend asked me to prom. I smirked and replied that Carrie would be a more interesting prom date.

However, if I find that book on eBay or AbeBooks, I will hunt him down like Annie Wilkes and bury him in the Pet Sematary.

Ferris Wheel and the Stop at the Top

Joanne Costantino

I love Ferris wheels. The best part for me about the Ferris wheel ride is the stop at the top. As each passenger gets off or on and each car inches its way around, I can't wait for the stop at the top. It is a view of the world below that I find simply fascinating.

It never occurred to me in my young excitement that my happy anticipation of climbing slowly up and around and stopping here and there could be anxiety for someone else.

My husband hates heights. On one of our early dates, we went to a carnival. I wanted to ride the Ferris wheel. In his eagerness to be gallant, he did get on the ride. But, on the way up, as I described the stop at the top, he told me how nervous this stuff made him. He was petrified of heights. I really couldn't understand his fear until we held hands. His was drenched with nervous sweat. He really hated that slow climb to the top but was willing and ready to do it with me and for me.

If I had to pinpoint a moment when I was sure he was a keeper, it wouldn't be that first ride on the Ferris wheel. It was the second one. It was his idea. I wouldn't think to ask him to suffer through something that made him so uneasy. The second Ferris wheel ride was on a much bigger Ferris wheel with a much longer stop at the top. His palms still dripped with nervous sweat, but I held his hand just a little tighter, in love and happy that I had someone who would do something that made me happy even if it gave him gross sweaty palms and made him almost sick to his stomach. What a guy!

Bless the Ice Cream

Ginger Graziano

Bless the ice cream, the sacrament of our time together. Bless St. Ben and St. Jerry and Jerry with his Cherry.

Bless the nights on the couch hanging out with my children in Sea Cliff, each with our own pint softening before us. Jeremy's was chocolate chip, each chip slowly dislodged from the frozen cream, popped into his mouth. Jenny preferred Mint Oreo, holding the frosty container as the ice melted and pooled in her lap, and me, New York Super Fudge Chunk, savoring every bite, holding it in my mouth until it ran cool down my throat.

No one talked as we sat on the couch, dipping spoonfuls of joy and licking the spoon, eating until we could hear the scrape of metal against empty. Blessed cows, with their rich cream and, oh, yes, chocolate which takes away all pain and nuts crunching between my teeth, releasing their flavor.

Jenny sighed, put down the spoon. "Remember when you brought home ice cream and the tops of the containers were already melting? Remember how you ate the soft top layer on each container before you even put it into the freezer?"

"After hours of shopping, it was my reward."

We had an unspoken rule in our house. Whoever didn't finish their pint in two days was just about saying, "It's up for grabs." Most of the time, it didn't last the first day.

Longing

Ginny Martin Fleming

Longing, longing, longing for connection and solitude simultaneously during these menopausal years of empty nesting challenges. Who am I, now that day-to-day mothering has left its uncomfortable void? I facebook to see photos of my daughter drinking at the latest sorority cocktail party, her smile not fooling me, for I know her. I am her. She is me. We both long for something we cannot even name. Something elusive, yet right in front of us. And so we live our lives with masks of confidence, successful to the outside world, beautiful to the men who love us, loved us, will love us, as we struggle to love ourselves.

Longing, longing, longing for a mother's lap to crawl into, to cry into, to collapse into, forgetting pride and fear and settling into the pain of loneliness inside our busy, smiling lives. Longing to stop the madness, to escape into our authentic selves, into each other maybe?

Pride, pride, her stubborn pride, so cruel, so harsh, as she willfully puts up that cold exterior. I did not raise her like that. No, she did that on her own when the hormones raged at fourteen, fifteen, sixteen, pushing me away, kicking me in the maternal gut, slapping me with her hateful words, flashing those stone cold, coal dark eyes, like daggers plunging into my crying soul. I had to stop the madness, kick her out of my soft mother's womb just as doing so broke open my wounded heart. This child of mine I'd rocked and nurtured, my "hip baby" until she was way older than the norm, her slight, lanky, delicate body perched awkwardly on my left hip, the one that gives me trouble now, just as my joints scream to walk without fear. My boundaries are better now. I can hear her moody tones without leaking too much life force. Slowly I am healing, despite yearning to hug this sweet baby adult daughter to my breast every single day.

Author's Note: For the record, time has healed the wounds. She is back; we are back. Thanks be to God!

On the
Map

...the journey toward
claiming our creative
expression is also the
journey toward
freeing our soul.

PTM

. . . .

Cantina Don Juan

Suzanne Blievernicht

Twin guitars pester *poco-a-poco*
cadence from flaming strings
entice the clicking echoes of ebony heels
from the cool darkness of her hiding place.
Quickened fingers excite the crescendo in syncopation
with the seductive pulse of clapping palms and castanets
cheers of anticipation electrify spoons
clinking the beat
on icy porcelain blooms of sangria pitchers.
A single klieg ignites the Chimera
its arc invading the shadows as
a whirling Maya emerges into the smoky haze
teases the ruffled red chiffon above her ankles
to a hint of calf encased in fishnet.
"Brava! Brava!"
cajoles the faux tortoise shell comb from her hair
and releases black ravens
to the orbiting edges
of her dervish.

"Más! Más!"

Flashing eyes of coal and languid lids
frolic with puckered cherry lips
a coquette behind the scarlet fan
she coaxes into full bloom
amid roars of expectation
casts it into the sea of voyeurs.
She spins and dips between tables

meeting and retreating
from hunger-glazed eyes
deftly dodging furtive gropes.
A seamless leap levitates her to a chair
en route to the tabletop refuge
she flees the surly stenches of
cigars, stale beer, testosterone
soars to the summit of the mesa, and slips
into dreams
of midnight
and

a

bath.

Midsummer Nights in Georgia

Suzanne Blievernicht

Supper completed around the metal kitchen table
leftovers stored in the ice box
dishes on the drainboard
Grandmother's apron laid on her chair back
ritual movement to the front porch
Grandfather retiring to his wicker rocker
silently signaled that day was done.

She climbed up close to the grandmother
in the swing that was too high
for her bare feet to touch the floor
as the elder tirelessly pumped it
into mesmerizing motion.

Darkness summoned a mysterious maestro
who stepped up to the podium
raised his baton and coaxed
a cacophony of cricket and cicada instruments
chirping and scratching their strident treble choruses
with the rocker stroking the bass
from wooden boards underneath

as the swing chains creaked their rhythms
into the audience of the night
beckoning explosions of lightning bugs
punctuated by the red glow
of the grandfather's Pall Mall inhalations
casting their tiny strobes into the shadows.

It was the same symphony each night
of stories that never grew old
easily mined from grandparents
who never seemed young.

The Irish Yankee grandfather told tales
of green and rocky coasts of family lands,
potato famine casualties and survivors who fled Erin,
ancestors on stormy seas,
immigrant Gloucester fishermen
straining against the wind and the wet
to haul in from briny depths
their brimming lobster traps
and
in his native Salem
a stone's throw from his First Communion site
incantation and spell casting women
burned at stakes
torched by fear, gossip, ignorance.

The Georgia peach grandmother gathered
recollections from her mother
of when General Sherman's troops
on his march to the sea
came calling
how the child's great grandmother
and her teenage sisters
rocked in wicker chairs and swung on rope hung swings
fanning themselves in the midsummer heat
on the plantation porch in Neal, Georgia
and giggled fearlessly
in innocent and dangerous flirtations
with the handsome Yankee soldiers

in shiny black boots who loitered with them
before pillaging
silver, trinkets, chickens
and any treasures not secretly buried
in the fields
on an anxious moonless night
by her father
and a trusted slave
and cantered away with cherished ancestral quilts
that flapped under saddles as cushions
for their ponies' aching backs
charging up the dusty road
to Atlanta
to set it ablaze.

The swinging lulled her to sleep
safely snuggled against the soft pillow
of the grandmother's bosom,
the movement in her dreams
the gentle rise and fall
of dories waltzing on moonlit oceans
and
the undulating rhythm
of a roan rocking horse
carried her across verdant pastures
to far away cities
where flames glowed
against nocturnal skies
as dark as black boot polish.

Her Cows Got into His Strawberry Patch

Jeanette Reid

Was it the scent that drew them in,
the sweetish tang, heads raised,
soft nostrils flaring?

Did brown bored eyes behold
the berry-red, those rows and rows
of foliage, fresh for taking?

Was *straw* the word they heard
that set saliva dripping,
graceful tails to twitching?

Or the sheer impulse to lumber
through a weakened fence,
to trample life so delicately aligned,
so ripened and desired.

An hour's frolic undetected,
dread e-coli now suspected.

The Bed

Betsy Fletcher

Dancing in darkness
Sweet chocolate earth cloak
Root and rhizome
Wild and tame
Entwined, restless
The annual tryst

Pigitaria fingers Lady Iris
Underground
Loamy, moist, fertile
Side by side
Blade to blade
They ascend
The rock border is of no consequence
Noxious ritual
Prevails

Her beauty, his roguish mystery
The attraction
Their rush to the sun
His need to stubbornly wrap, possess,
Choke her last breath
With his own triumphant exhalation
Bold and strong, each
Holding ground
Green, enmeshed

True
White knight trowel
Digs
Deep
Gently lifts Pigitaria
Out
For one more season

Breathless,
Lady Iris adjusts her petticoats, proper again
Smiles, nods, faces the garden
Dreams of another early spring
Dance

Author's Note: Pigitaria is the genus for crabgrass.

*Power
of Place*

*We relive the moment when
a ray of sun through the morning
fog transmutes a single maple leaf to
gold or when the sacred smell
of silence inside an old barn speaks
the stories of earth and time,
of love and loss. In each of these
moments, the heart splits open.
We can do nothing but watch
our love spill out upon the ground.*
                                        PTM

. . . .

Thoughts on a Morning Walk

Kathy Sievert

The field lies fallow, good enough pasture for
an old horse, sway-backed, dull-coated,
lazily grazing in the sparse grass.

Time diminishes the capacity to change.
Fresh starts shrivel when there's not enough light.
Annuals make more sense for the garden, one season's burst of
color.
Perennials presume too much future.
These days what's possible is measured by how much time is left.

Every goodbye means something now.
"Bye-bye," her grandchildren say to her,
one of the first words they learn to speak.
Time will teach them the finality of loss.

Trudging up the steep path,
she plucks a dandelion stem,
blows the furry cap of spores
and sends them spinning in the wind,
each one a wish for something more.

Third Day of Spring

Jeannette Reid

Third day of spring
and winter back again—sharp wind,
sleety rain. Daffodils, hyacinths push up
undaunted. I want to rake my fingers
through loose dirt.
Instead I kneel beside the hearth, turn
palms towards the flames.
The angst of spring—new life, old bones—
each calling for attention.
Fire that's self-consuming.
Plants reckless, weary of their graves.
They tell me ashes mixed with earth will feed
the roots, produce abundant flowering.
I want the blooms, but not the wilting blossoms,
the fire without the ashes.

These Mountains Here

Alicia Porterfield

The mountains blow down their secrets on me, a sharp chill wind, scraping its story on my skin, a tattoo of bad endings and bloody triumphs and anger that festers up and rots away the good, growing up and over whatever hope is left after the fire burns through the first time.

> The winter sun can't overcome that kind of bitter wind; it can try to press its rays in close around, a cape of warmth against what blows, but it is too tired up there in that cold wintry sky,

>> And I'm too far down in this valley, low down here in the tunnel the wind carves, alone and deep and too long from the sun.

These mountains here are ancient, so old they have layer on layer of grief in their thin soil, hanging on, hugging that stone tight, afraid it might blow away.

> So the stories lay thick and tangled in that little strip of soil, all pressed down and stepped on 'til they start to coil up like snakes, waiting for the next fragile foot to bite, sink down into, delighted with the pain they've caused, so glad to be living again, noticed and heard, after all that thin, pressed silence.

>> Someone has to listen now. Someone has no choice. Truths get told at some point, especially the ones we wish would stay quiet forever. Stories long to be heard. It's what they're meant for and they'll cry out, even from stone, if they're not.

So be careful up on those mountains. The rock you rest on halfway up may be thick with memories you don't want to know. If you brush by a tree trunk where an old truth waits, clinging to the bark, it might latch onto your sleeve and soak right in before you even hear it whisper.

And it will wait for the right moment to unravel there and spool down into your life to say what it has been living to say all these years, all these years.

When the wind blows in these mountains, I feel the edges of the stories rushing by.

The Ocean

Ginny Fleming

The ocean is a gentle, soothing lullaby on a sweltering afternoon. Its gritty liquid smells salty in my frizzy curls, lapping melted sherbet on my parched feet. The ocean's endless beauty stretches out like an infinite red carpet, leading to heaven and to heaven only knows where, connecting my tightened heart to relaxed peace.

Hurricane Coming

Joy Wallace Dickinson

Mary looked out the window. She could see the high branches of the trees starting to sway in the wind. The radio had said the storm would arrive in the early morning, but maybe it was moving faster—maybe it would hit them in the middle of the night, when they couldn't see. Maybe they wouldn't be ready.

She worried. Hank was always so casual about the storms, but there was a lot to do to get ready. Their neighbors were already getting out their hurricane shutters, and Mary thought she should at least get the candles organized and make sure she knew where the canned beans were.

"It's nothing, Mary," Hank had said. "You know how those weather people on the radio like to make a fuss. It rains a lot—so what? The garden could use it."

Mary frowned. "Mrs. MacGruder down the street told me that one summer a hurricane smashed a big tree limb right through their roof, and they had a real mess on their hands, water everywhere," she said. "Look at the folks next door—they've been putting up shutters since lunchtime."

"Aw, that guy's an old lady," said Hank. "Just moved down from Kansas last year—thinks a hurricane's like a tornado—if people built cellars in Florida, he'd be digging one to hide in."

"Well, I hear some people are building cellars," Mary said, "for bomb shelters."

"Exactly," said Hank. "One of them A-bombs is something to worry about. I figure ol' Fidel has stacks of them down there in Cuba. But a hurricane? Come on, Mary—it's just a big windstorm. No A-bomb."

Mary looked up again at the high branches of the old oaks. She looked at the tall palms, swaying in the rising wind, their green plumes waving. They seemed to be waving to her, speaking in some secret tree language, as if they knew trouble was coming. Maybe the trees could feel trouble across the miles, hear signals riding in from the far-away air over the Gulf. This one was different, the high branches seemed to be saying to her, *Get ready, Mary, get ready.* This one was more than a big storm. This one would make even old Fidel shudder down there in Cuba.

Malaspina Strait

Cindy Peterson

Gripping the tiller in the predawn light, I glanced below. I could see my crew slipping deeper into their bunks trying to drown out the roar of the diesel engine. I pulled the cabin doors shut and closed the hatch to quiet my own world. It was flat calm. I pointed my bow towards the west, gradually moving away from the protection of the steeply forested mountains that had watched over us so far.

I pulled my down jacket closer, shivering in the cool morning air, watching the sunlight touch the tips of the peaks with brilliance, measuring its slow creep down the hillsides towards the emerald green waters. The potential of a sunny, warm day lent me courage and excitement. Today was a new step for me. I would be taking my first trip out of the protection of Jervis Inlet and making my way up the more exposed waters of Malaspina Strait.

I chose an early start for a reason. I knew I would be alone, giving me time to grapple with the fear I felt about the day's journey. I did not want my friends to see this fear. It was buried beneath the jokes, the teenage bravado, the daily dose of cold Canadian brew. I faced it only when I was alone. I remember this dawn departure now many years later because of what I experienced on a morning so breathtakingly beautiful, it was transcendent.

I seemed to be the only one on those calm misty waters that morning. The sun rose gradually over the mountains behind me, its first beams shooting horizontally between the gaps in the high peaks. Golden hues lit the scenery around me. The cold crisp air invoked a mist from the calm surface that my bow cut through and pushed away. My stern wake trailed behind me in a meandering line with perfect patterns of waves making a "v" shape far into the distance. Holding that tiller in my hand, breathing that cool morning air, surrounded by the majesty and the mystery of such wild places, I felt fully alive. Adventure and challenge were before me and so was God. His presence all around me. I knew the moment was shared with Him, my creator, imprinting in me a way of being, a way of life that would captivate me always.

Eventually, my reverie passed as I began to notice signs of a change. Nearing the end of the long channel, I approached the broad open waters of Malaspina Strait. The wind was quickening. The waves taking shape and force. Clearly, despite blue skies, the sea was restless. I felt a shiver of dread as I recalled some of the bad Strait crossings I had been through as a kid. The handful I had experienced were indelibly etched in my memory. This day felt like a test. Strait crossings were like the proving ground, and this was my first solo. It would be an education.

I learned that day that a calm sunny morning in the shelter of a protected inlet does not necessarily guarantee a safe, calm voyage throughout the day.

I learned that day that tide running against rising wind is a deadly combination, generating waves that no change of course can accommodate. Rounding the headland, to get out into the Strait, I was forced to steer directly into the boiling, confused seas. The twenty-six-foot sailboat began to pitch and roll violently. It was all I could do to hold myself in place to steer.

I learned that day that a seasick crew member won't stay below in the safety of the cabin no matter how miserable it is in the cock-pit.

I learned that day to brace myself in such a way that I could hold the heavy pull of the tiller and the back of my friend's jeans as she vomited over the side.

Soaked with sea water, shivering with cold, we beat our way up the Sunshine Coast. My sense of helplessness felt overwhelming, terrifying.

After an hour of focusing only on each oncoming wave, I glanced at my white-faced companion, now pressed against the leeward wall of the cabin staring over the stern.

"You okay?" I asked.

She mustered a smile. "I'll live," she laughed. "I think it's getting a little better."

Our course now pointing more directly into the wind, the waves took a more predictable pattern. The others climbed out of the cabin. The sun glittered in the spray flying over the bow. Fear's adrenaline turned to wild playfulness. Finding handholds on the front deck, my crew rode each wave as swashbuckling adventurers—singing and shouting as the white water washed over them.

I marveled from my place at the tiller, grateful. How quickly things changed.

Once

Maggie Wynne

I saw God
dance down by the depot,
incarnate in a T-shirt
orange as October.
He wore cut offs, scuffed shoes caked
with the dear dirt of play.
Six going on seven,
his quick feet (they cannot stay still)
moved to the rumbling rattle,
the roar of number 474.
He grinned, delighted
by the shrill whistle's shock,
split the blue of Saturday's tender sky
with surprise.

Just another small town,
downtown day stretched, yawned,
reluctantly woke. Merchants
along Cherry Street
grumbled as they counted out change.
All the while my little friend jumped up
and down. He
boogied to the song
silver rails sing as each car clatters by,
proud with freight.

But oh! Wonder smiles beneath
a freckled nose, then waves goodbye, red caboose,
goodbye.

Strange Things Pass

Joy Wallace Dickinson

Strange things pass us in the night, thought Emily, as she looked down at the kitchen floor. Scuttling past her foot was the largest insect she had ever seen.

"Good Lord, what is this?" she called to Milton, who was unloading her bags on the back porch. He opened the screen door and came inside.

"Ah, now, that would be what some folks call a roach in Florida, Miz Emily, but others call them palmetto bugs. Don't worry—no matter how clean you keep a house, they have a way of getting inside and prowling around at night."

The thing on the floor looked like something time forgot. Emily imagined her new kitchen, the black and white squares of its linoleum floor cheery by day, but after the lights went out, home to scores of these flat, brown, winged creatures. She saw them marching across the floor in formation—insect armies that clashed by night. Could they fly?

Then, before she knew what was happening, Milton swooped down one large hand and opened the screen door with the other. He hurled the creature into the damp night in a single, seamless motion.

She gasped.

"Nothin' to worry about," Milton said. "You're gonna like Florida fine." He went to the kitchen sink and calmly washed his hands with Fels-Naptha. "Now," he said, "let me get the rest of those bags from the car."

Sally and Tammi at the Suds and Spin

Alicia Porterfield

Sally looked up from her novel as Tammi slouched in front of the plate glass windows, toting a basket full of dirties. The girl sported pajama bottoms and a man's cheap undershirt. *At least she's dressed up,* Sally mused. The rounding of Tammi's five-month pregnancy was finally starting to show on her thin seventeen-year-old frame. Sally sighed, dreading the glimpse of dead-end life coming in the door. *Okay, Prophet Jeremiah,* she told herself, *stop being so doom and gloom.*

Tammi backed in the door, pushing it open with her rear end. "Hey," she grunted at Sally, slapping the basket on the community table and starting to sort. She went through her clothes with the same enthusiasm she did everything else: slowly plodding and resentful, as if the shape of the world was never to her liking. Sally watched, strangely fascinated. Tammi turned suddenly—or as suddenly as she did anything—and caught Sally staring. "You got any of that, like, stain remover I can use? I forgot mine and Teri's brat done spit up his sweet potatoes all down my Bennett Brothers signed concert T-shirt."

Sally snapped into action. "Sure. It's over here where Mr. Bill left it." She scurried over, feeling old and nosy, delivering the economy-sized, lightning red bottle of stain remover that had been sitting just two washers down from where they stood. Tammi received it with her usual gratefulness and excitement, which was almost none.

"Thanks," she heaved in a sigh.

"How are you feeling?" Sally ventured, wiping down her side of the table with a spare paper towel.

"Uhhh . . . fine. A little tired, but the woman at the clinic says that should get better now I'm in my second trimester." Tammi sniffed and rubbed her nose with the back of her hand. Kept sorting.

Sally couldn't help herself. "And your GED class? How's that going?"

"Oh, I had to drop out of that class. I needed to watch Traci's baby on Tuesday nights 'cause she got moved to the evening shift at the Tank and Tummy, and Mama calls bingo that night. So that didn't work out."

"Huh." Sally rubbed the table more vigorously, trying to think of something constructive to say. When the third of three teen-age-mom sisters drops her GED class to watch her one-year-old nephew so her sister can work a job at a convenience store, what do you say? They don't cover that in most divinity school classes. Sally kept scrubbing harder. And harder.

She couldn't help herself. Again. "Wonder when they'll offer it again?"

"I dunno."

Sally moved to wiping down the nearest washer to keep her hands busy so they wouldn't grab the girl and shake her. Sally knew instinctively from the anger welling up that she was over-invested, which would lead to being over-opinionated—and then to a night full of should-have-said scenarios. *You can't do her work for her,* her former mentor, Chaplain Davis, whispered in her ear.

Shut up, Sally whispered back. *Anyway, what am I going to say? Get your GED so you can end up managing a laundromat like me?*

Sally shook her head to clear out the voices. Still scrubbing away, she was now on washer number two.

This girl is God's precious child, beloved, some ancient saint murmured from a book Sally had read years ago.

Too bad she can't see it, Sally agreed.

Too bad you can't either, the voice popped back.

Fine, then. FINE!

"You okay with giving up the class?"

Pause. Sigh. "Yeah. Don't know as I could pass it anyways. The GED, I mean."

"Why not?"

"I suck at math. Always have."

"Me, too . . . but I bet there's someone in town who could help you with the math part. If you wanted, I mean."

"I dunno. I dunno what I want."

First clear statement I've ever heard from her. "You don't know what you want."

Tammi was done sorting and shuffled over to a now-sparkling washer number one. "I never been real good at nothin'. Bad at school. Can't sing. Can't dance. Not good at sports. I mean, I don't know what I want to do."

"Sounds like you don't know what you can do."

"I can't do nothin'. 'Cept take care of people's kids. I'm pretty good at that. Been babysittin' since I was twelve. Kids like me, I guess." Tammi shrugged.

So you get pregnant at 17? "I think that's a pretty big talent—being good with kids. There's a lot of people out there who aren't."

"I dunno. What can you do with that?"

"Teach school. Teach preschool. Work at Headstart. Be a teacher's assistant. Work at a daycare or day camp. Be a nanny. Be a social worker who specializes in children. Major in child development." Sally stopped herself and took a deep breath. *I can't care more about this than she does.*

Tammi heaved a sigh and started throwing clothes in the machine. The stale cigarette smoke coating them wafted to where Sally stood, shredded paper towel in hand. She thought of the babies and winced. *One thing at a time, sweet Jesus.*

Tammi kept feeding clothes into the washer, her mouth hanging open a bit. Sally suddenly had an image of the entire family as the subject of a trashy talk show. The three sisters would each have a baby on a jutting hip, like Watkins' own little reality TV show.

"Tammi, I think you've got more going for you than you know."

Tammi looked up at Sally blankly, her acne-pocked cheeks

looking nothing like those paintings of the Virgin Mary.

God's beloved, the saint whispered.

Just then, a few lines from the song "Redneck Woman" flew from a passing car into the laundromat.

"I love that song!" Tammi blurted, looking the most excited Sally had ever seen her. "I'm a redneck woman, I ain't no high class broad . . .," she twanged, shimmying the bottle of stain remover in her hand.

The myth and reality are two different things. The real thing was standing right there doling out dollar-store washing powder, her pregnant belly bumping up against the machine's cool front. The real thing talked about herself as if she wasn't even on her own team, as if everything had already dead ended for her, as if that old trailer with its border of plastic flowers was the best she'd ever do.

Sally shuddered and squatted down to wipe off the front of a dryer on the other aisle.

Tammi settled the lid on her machine and looked up, spotting Sally's back across the way. "So, Pastor Sally, didn't I see you with Mr. Jed at the football game last Friday?"

Sally froze, resting her forehead on the dryer. *Oh, dear God, I've become Watkins' own reality TV show.*

If I Can't Shoot My Rifle

Nancy Newlin

Walking out into the hay field in back of my house on a cold, quiet January afternoon, I heard a car start up with a loud roar. I turned and looked in the direction of the sound. A dark blue Volvo sedan came swiftly down the hill and across the field towards me and my dogs. The driver's side window was down. The car stopped right by us.

"Hi, Rick."

"Tracey, I'll have to ask you to stay off my property," he said, without any congenial inquiry into the large sling I was wearing on my left arm.

Taken by surprise after his long-ago invitation to walk around the perimeter of his hay field—which he mowed partly for that purpose—I said, "But you said that I could walk around this field."

"Well, things have changed."

"They have?" I thought he was going to tell me that he had sold that ten-acre parcel as he had said last summer, when he and his wife were drinking wine with me on my back porch.

"Someone complained to the sheriff about my shooting off my rifle."

"It wasn't me and I don't know who it was," I said, and raised my right hand in scout's honor.

"Whoever it was, I don't know why they made such a fuss. I only get out my rifle for some target practice every three years or so. So I figure that if I can't use my property the way I want to, then no one else gets to use it either. And besides I don't want to be responsible if you should hurt yourself walking around out here."

"Oh, okay, Rick. Sorry to hear that, but thanks for letting me know." The dogs and I turned around and started back home. Rick made a quick U-turn and sped back up the hill to his house.

As we walked away, I thought I probably did know who called the sheriff and why, and because of that call, our enjoyment of that long walk is over—dammit! I'd seen and heard him out there once last fall doing target practice with a large and very noisy rifle—he only took about five shots at a target on a large dead tree—and I knew what his rights were to do just that. He's obviously mad as hell that someone called the sheriff. The "I don't want to be responsible if you get hurt" is just an excuse. He'll never back off from being mad about this. I bet his wife is none too happy about him letting his anger out on me. Up till now I thought we had a really nice neighborly relationship.

A few weeks later, high winds blew another neighbor's dried-out Christmas tree from their yard out into the field. My first thought was to haul it out of the field back into their yard. My second thought was to contact my neighbor about retrieving their tree.

Then I remembered Rick's demand that I stay out of his field. So I left it there.

He'd better not call me about that Christmas tree, I thought. *If he does, I'll say, "Rick, it's not my tree. I really wanted to be neighborly and fetch it out of your hay field, but you told me in no uncertain terms to stay out."*

More likely, he'll see it out there, get out his utility vehicle, charge down the hill to pick it up, take it to his dump pile, and drive back home swearing all the while about that Christmas tree being one more violation of his property rights.

Identity

When I write, I understand it is
myself that will be revealed—not
the self I have constructed to feel safe
in my world, but a self I do not fully
know. The promise of adventurous
discovery provides both the impetus
to move forward and the urge to run
away. The trust is that whichever
way I run, I will meet myself and
the unknown.

PTM

. . . .

Pheromones

Deborah Cantrell

Darlene Doe Hawkins McCabe Brewer Simpson was tall, beautiful, and very sexy. Whatever IT was, she had IT. And she knew it. When Darlene walked in the bar, the male skulls swirled in unison, like a herd of hapless antelope sniffing a lioness. Darlene had perfected the slow, undulating, pelvis-protruding glide, like the glamorous movie stars in the old movies. Her musky perfume wafted invitingly in the air around her as she slid, bottom first, into the corner booth. Her seductive entrance was all a part of her practiced, nonchalant allure.

Darlene knew how to work the crowd from her little table in the corner. She made men tremble, transfixed and drooling, when she performed her special lipstick trick. With her perfectly manicured nails, she calmly pulled her shiny, black, square lipstick tube from her purse and gently removed the cap. Then she ever so gradually rolled the red, glossy cylinder to its full length, tilting her head and staring at it, as if she planned to eat it. She then, ever so slowly, adjusted it down just a tad, before placing the erect, red projectile to her lips. With one hand softly cradling the other to steady her aim, and her eyes half-closed, she applied the lipstick perfectly—first to the bottom lip and then to the top—all without a mirror. Darlene next moistened her crimson lips together and flicked her tongue tip gently around the inside edges, leaving her wet mouth slightly open. As she slowly retracted the lipstick back into the tube, her languid, green eyes surveyed the room to discreetly count the men fixated, enraptured, and gawking with slack jaws. This simple little routine could be counted on for a free drink or two.

Who knew? she thought. *Husband Number Four might be right there at the bar, staring at her with that half-drunk, slurpy, turned-on look in his eyes, ready to swan-dive off his stool.*

Darlene's current husband, Malcolm the computer genius, was trying her patience. He bought her this diamond necklace, a gold choker chain with a four-carat solitaire in the center. He expected her to wear it everywhere. "Now even drunk sons-of-bitches will be able to see this big baby, sparkling from way across the room in every dim-lit bar in the state of Mississippi and know you are taken! Problem solved." The big diamond chained around her neck was Malcolm Simpson's nerdy idea of a "hands-off" sign.

She touched the necklace, caressing the diamond with her long red nails, as she moved it around her neck to the back where her auburn hair hid it completely. Funny how that diamond grew smaller every day while the necklace grew heavier. It felt more and more like a real dog collar, a choke chain ready to be yanked on by an angry master. Not all chastity belts buckled around the waist.

Darlene decided, then and there, as a free drink arrived from an anonymous admirer, that the diamond necklace would be made into a bracelet. Mr. Husband-Man Number Four, she vowed, would buy her a proper ring, maybe a large ruby. Rubies are for women who are virtuous and pure in heart. It says so in the Bible. She did not yet own a single ruby. It was time, she thought, and smiled to herself, lifting her drink to toast the muses and fluttering her eyelashes at the older gentleman in the white linen suit.

Biker Babe

Cheryl Deitrich

In my next life, I want to be a biker babe with tattooed arms, strong thighs, tan freckled face, and dirty-blonde hair pulled back into a braid that goes down to my waist. I'll ride behind a long-haired, bearded dude, leaning into his back, arms encircling his beer gut. Sometimes I'll sit straight, hands and arms flung into the stinging wind. I'll drive my own chopper, too. I will not be careful or restrained or restricted.

When I'm a biker babe, I will not know what's on PBS, what NPR stands for, what the local fine arts cinema is showing. I will never use the word "cinema." I will not drink wine, eat food with foreign names, grill vegetables, sear or broil or cook at all. I will not recycle or volunteer or vote or march for peace or go to church. I will not turn on CNN or read newspapers.

I will not know about things that could be but are not now. Events will spring on me like surprises, far-off surprises. My world will be tiny and here. About other places, unknown people, I will not care. And, I will not feel guilty.

I will like movies with car chases and gory screamers and comedies where people fart. I will laugh really loud, with my mouth wide open and big "ha's" exploding out. My drinks will have screw tops, my food fried and served in paper. Maybe I'll smoke even inside houses and drink beer till I get a buzz on and sometimes use substances that are far worse. My body will be no temple but a house of pleasure. I will not try to live forever.

When I am a biker babe, I may wear a helmet occasionally, but never leathers, just jeans and a T-shirt that sits too tight on me. It will say "Made in the USA," with appropriate pictures. I will wear a jacket with chains in cold weather. I'll ride with a crew of good friends, bikers and babes. Some days, I'll drive off by myself for the joy of being just me and the bike. I will sing bawdy songs at the top of my voice. I will never be lonely.

I will roar forth with lusty pagan impulses and live a child's life with sweet abandon once again. I will careen around mountain curves tasting wildness. I will chase the sun west. I will rush into quiet camps with harsh clattering engine noises that shatter the peaceful silence into tinkling shards. I will destroy the hushed serenity. I will not worry about what people think. I will yell above the whispers. I will be heard.

In my next life, I will never be afraid. I will be a biker babe.

Change of Life

Kathleen Rada Boswell

I need to tell you the God's truth about menopause. They call it change of life, but they never mention the change of person that accompanies it. I used to be perfectly happy in my own skin. Not really ever too hot or too cold, kind of like Goldilocks, I always found the "just right." If I happened to hit the too hot or too cold I could always take off or conversely put on something and again experience equilibrium. But my friend, that changed a few years ago.

It was never mentioned, at least not in the reading material I glanced through while waiting for my yearly GYN exams, that this menopause stuff continued on and on and on. I may have experienced my last "time of the month" at fifty, but, believe me, for years before and now years after, this change just keeps on giving—for all the hot flashes I have had, I would think that the little pink bunny's batteries would have run out.

But then, this heat is not battery operated—it is heat that cannot be cooled down, kind of like Arkansas heat. It starts from the inside and comes boiling out as sweat from every single pore of your body. No matter how low the house thermostat is turned down. No matter that the rest of the family has on sweatshirts and their calves are cramping, you will not be cooled off. The perspiration will drip down the side of your face, bead up on your arms, make you look like you wet your pants, and fog up your reading glasses.

Oh, and this menopause can make you one angry middle-aged woman. I wondered what happened to the woman who could so easily "go with the flow," but when the flow stopped became a raving maniac. I tell you, I never pictured myself as the kind of woman who would hyperventilate and harshly berate a car-wash guy because he left a couple of smudges on the rearview mirror. But berate I did – this madwoman would take over my mind and then proceed to make a complete ass out of me. Then to add injury to insult, I felt no remorse; I was only further pissed off.

Oh, and let's talk about the weight gain. You are going along minding your own business and suddenly the scales start to creep up, but because you are so irritated at the entire world you will not notice it until you have gained the required fifteen to twenty pounds. The french fries that you never took notice of before, or at least could resist, now will call to you from several of the different fast food chains. I made it my personal mission to decide which ones were the best, only I never let *Consumer Reports* know. (By the way, McDonald's, but they must be hot out of the fryer. I took to lurking in the back of the store until I saw the fry cook add another batch.) It was so reminiscent of the Baskin-Robbins craving for Chocolate Almond ice cream when I was pregnant, only now I wasn't growing another person; I was just growing me.

Also be forewarned that at times your spouse or partner will look at you strangely but, out of fear, I am sure, say nothing. My husband had this "who is this woman?" stunned look on his face for most of about five years. Even my son and his friends, usually the thundering herd, tiptoed through the house for fear that I would pick up a wooden spoon and begin swatting them because they pissed me off about something. My usual ten-year-old-boy humor disappeared and farting was no longer funny.

So be forewarned. Yes, it will eventually end but ever soooo slowly. One day will go by and you will realize that you didn't pound on the car steering wheel once and you didn't mash every button on the telephone and start screaming when the automated operator said, "Press one for…" You will find yourself smiling at the checkout lady who is telling you to have a good day. You will feel better and, if you still have a husband after all of this, you may just be ready to outlive him.

70-Something

Mary Freen

I am 71 this year, no 72.
Never mind, I am happily confused and heels over head.
I met someone.
Yes, you know what I mean . . .
Someone.
And I'm just amazed that I,
content to be a widow and
finish the downslope in a twin-size bed,
I met someone—
not through a dating service,
not through any dot com,
but in the JC Penney on Bassington,
where he was shopping for his grandchild and I was shopping for
mine,
and we stood in line while the salesperson rung and then un-rung
two pillows king-size, one set of sheets king-size, one blanket
king-size,
and two bath towels, two hand towels and two wash cloths
because the customer had and then did not have
her credit card or cash or as it turns out her wallet.
We stood waiting and quite naturally began to chat
and the proverbial thing leading to,
we carried our bags, finally, to the food court and had coffee.
And the proverbial thing leading to, we agreed to meet again.
My proper self told my practical self the whole thing was once and
only,
but meeting begat meeting and polite smiles became flirtatious
laughter.
My practical self told my wishful self, "you are too old for this,"

but dinner and movie begat picnic at the beach,
and flirtatious laughter became suggestive looks.
My wishful self told my romantic self that kissing is like riding a
bike
and under the porch light, with Jasper barking at the window,
my romantic self told my proper self that love is wasted on the
young.
The wedding is next Saturday,
in the park next to the church across from JCPenney
where I am going now to buy sheets and pillows and
blankets king-size for our new bed.
Let me just check to be sure I have my wallet.

The Kata

Jennifer Lynn Browning

Before the *kata* begins, the sleeves are folds of silence. A bow and they wing up ready to fly. A punch and they bark attention. A kick and they float into the air, part of defense, part of deception. A turn and the sleeves fold left and right, silent still but guardians all the same—the stiff outer cuff, the softness of the material protecting, covering, softening the punches and blocks and kicks.

If only the sleeves could hold my mind in silence too, then I could fold my fears and insecurities and critics into silent bundles like I do my *gi* at the end of practice, securing it with my worn purple belt, waiting to be unfolded at some other time. If I could do that, my mind would get out of my way and when I was called on to do an art or defense or kick or punch, I wouldn't have the second or two of blank mind, the flight part of fight or flight, always my first response. Then I would stand confident and sure, folded in the silence of calm and surety. Then, I would feel my muscles stretch and coil, my breath move in and out in intentional ways, my arms and legs would lose their awkwardness and timidness, and my kata would flow smoothly one move to the other.

I like the silence of the solo kata. The way each move can be isolated but also combined. The way my arms and legs move as though they actually do know what they are doing. When I do the kata with my eyes closed, it becomes a dance and I am balanced without sight, centered without sound. I am controlled and controlling in a positive sense of both of those words. I can feel the ground below me, the air around me, and the folds of silence that embrace me. My mind empties and I am there—in the moment. Sure and assured. I come to the end of the movement and, as I come to a stop, my sleeves again move into their folds of silence, the cuffs protecting, the material covering, the white, pure and serene. The kata becomes my sitting meditation, and I am ready.

Letting Go

Mary Freen

The movers will be here tomorrow to load the truck. It's time, but I have trouble letting go. My sister Ann says, "Just look forward," as if it's that easy. "It's like jumping in the pool when you know it's going to be cold. Remember how we used to pretend we were penguins? We dove in head first. Just move on and don't look back."

Easy for Ann to say. She's lived in the same house for thirty-two years, but I followed her advice, at least I tried. Sometimes half-heartedly, but yes, I moved on. We had been in Port Hampton for about a year when some business brought us back to Edgewater one day. George had a meeting downtown so I decided to stop in The Tin Roof, a little antique shop I used to visit.

Just inside the door stood a tea cart with a brass frame and glass shelves. The frame was dull with tarnish and its wheels were well scuffed. How many dozens of times had it been rolled between the kitchen nook and dining room? How many large family gatherings and holiday dinners had it served? I knew it immediately, for it had been my parents' tea cart and had lived under the counter next to the refrigerator through all the years of my childhood. It was where Mom set the overflow of dishes from Thanksgiving and Christmas dinners, where Dusty, our cocker spaniel, took refuge during the afternoon thunderstorms that happened almost daily every June.

I had seen it among the garage sale items at my mother's place years ago. My father had passed away a dozen years before and my sister Rhoda had finally convinced Mom to sell the four-bedroom house and move in with her family. It was a decision we all cheered, but I remembered it now with a better understanding of how hard that new beginning had been for Mom. Except for her bedroom furniture, she let go of most everything else, happy to have us kids pick any pieces we wanted. I had always liked that tea cart and I thought about taking it and fixing it up. But I was so busy in those days, when would I ever get around to it?

I wasn't there the day of the sale, but Ann said a woman had come early and bought the cart and a number of other items. And that was that. Ten years ago and fifty miles away. Now it stood here in front of me just a couple of miles from my old home.

It was a sign. But what kind of sign? Was my angel tempting my resolve to let go of the past? Or was she offering me a gift, this beat up little tea cart full of memories.

So began the back and forth with myself. Where will I put it? Do I really need it? I have the perfect place for it. How will I get it home? Of course I don't need it. Can it even be fixed up? That piece there looks a little bent. What will George say? Thank goodness we drove the van. Oh, George won't mind. He knows I have trouble letting go.

Sagua

Heidi Stewart

She stood on the edge of the rock, surveying the valley below, her long black hair gently blowing in the wind. Above her on the ledge, wolf stood silently watching. A medicine woman, surveying the land of the Creator, looking for a sign of green, the first sign of medicine for the spring, below her, she saw a hunting party searching for wild game. She backed away from the edge of the rock to the cave, where she could watch them unobserved.

This was a time for her to be alone, to reflect upon the harsh winter. So many lives had been lost to the cold and lack of food. Last fall the hunting had been sparse and even less game had come through during the winter than usual. She had nurtured her people with the plants and herbs she had gathered—mushrooms, comfrey, witch hazel, ginseng root, willow bark—but nothing could take the place of a strong stew. Many babies passed over to the Great Spirit, elders, too. Now, spring had finally arrived, and she had fixed a tonic for them with fresh stinging nettles found growing next to the creek, and they had all performed a ceremony for life and abundance in this time of the new moon. Now the men were out hunting. She smiled as one of them gave a "Whoop!" and held up a wild turkey.

When Sagua began gathering her herbs each spring, she would note where the ginseng and cohosh were sprouting up from the ground with their shiny green serrated edges unfolding. She would sit with them and get to know them and listen to their stories of the earth mother. She would hear their songs and hum them. Then she would move on to the wild cherry trees and check to see if the sap had risen enough for her to strip the bark from them, filling the air with the sweet smell of cherry. From the bark, she would make medicine to soothe her people's coughs.

Today, upon leaving the cave, she sat on a rock beside the waterfall below and as the water rushed down the upper creek into a pool, she noticed a few trout hiding under the bank close to the edge. Setting down her work, she quietly reached behind her, pulled an arrow out of her deerskin bag and set it to her bow. Drawing the arrow tightly against the gut of the bow, she aimed and set it soaring toward its intended target. Jumping up to grab her arrow with its catch before she lost it down the fast moving current, she cried, "Ayahh—fresh fish to eat tonight," as her mouth began to water. Thanking Creator, she made her way back up the ridge with her catch.

Owning Self

Within the spaciousness of the belly

is truly where the Muse resides,

not hanging around the rafters or

perched on our shoulder

whispering in our ear. The more

we bring our awareness

to this place, the more we notice

the tension there and elsewhere

in the body.

PTM

. . . .

Spasmodic Dysphonia's Gifts

Kimberly Childs

All people narrate their life story; this is part of what makes us human. Answering the simple question of "how was your day" reaffirms our presence in the world. I cannot do this. Speech is difficult for me due to an unusual neurological condition called spasmodic dysphonia. My voice is trapped in my throat by spasming and paralyzed vocal folds. I struggle to produce a strangled sigh that is difficult to understand. This is isolating and just plain inconvenient. I can't ask for directions or tell you my concerns. My phone seldom rings and an operator must relay my telephone messages. I live in an island of quiet that sometimes feels blessedly peaceful but at other times is lonely.

Thank goodness, I discovered meditation when I was young. For many years, I have been practicing Zen Buddhism in the gentle tradition of Thich Nhat Hanh. I go on extended silent retreats where there is no demand to make sounds. I love the intimacy of no speech. People reveal themselves in the way they sit, open the door and walk through. I can be with you in the fullness of present moment. In this environment, my being expands to incorporate everything. The woods, sky, pebbles under my feet are who I am.

At the final lunch of a silent retreat, everyone bursts into noisy conversation, exchanging details of their busy lives. As the hullaba-loo mounts, I am revealed as a permanent non-speaker. I struggle not to feel excluded, but people are caught up in their talk and don't notice me. I live in enforced Noble Silence 24/7.

Noisy restaurants and roaring cars exacerbate my situation. Alone in a crowd is a feeling I know well. The other day during a hike I was not able to speak freely while others chatted, and sud-denly my heart cried out. I wanted so desperately to be heard and to engage. I felt like a little girl again, back at my mother's parties with the adults holding forth while I was invisible. There was nothing I could do . . . except choose, then and now. As a child I turned to make-believe. As an adult I ask: do I allow myself to be overwhelmed by self-pity or do I follow my breath and smile with compassion for the pain in my heart?

On that hiking day, I turned to my Buddhist practice and nature. Dropping to the back of the line, I grew quiet within myself. I followed my breath and felt my feet kissing the earth. I let my ears open to the softest, most distant sounds: the staccato clatter of a woodpecker's excavations, the soughing wind in the trees, and the muffled sound of my own footsteps. At one point I saw the flash of a scarlet tanager and with every step I became increasingly aware of my old friends the trout lilies, bloodroot, and violets. As I see, I am seen—and I am comforted. I am home in the here and the now.

It took me a long time to appreciate spasmodic dysphonia's many gifts. Only when I could no longer speak did I begin to listen. I hear what a person is saying without planning my response or being impelled to carry the conversational thread. I am free to step outside social norms and enjoy the intimacy of the moment; the light caressing your hair, the joy in your tone, simply being with you. When I do speak, I limit my words to the pith and that gives them power.

Hearing is a path in itself. I discovered ears are deep receptacles that link me to the present moment. When I meditate, I invite spaciousness by listening to the farthest sound I can hear. I experience how silence surrounds and gives birth to sound. In pristine silence is the potentiality for everything.

Birds have become my passion. I hear their amazing variety of calls and can identify many by ear. Each spring, the return of the warblers to our forests thrills me. I walk slowly in the cathedral of trees allowing the songs of my friends to echo in my heart.

Possessing a childlike whisper of a voice forced me to feel and embrace my shame, that I am the other, handicapped and vulnerable. That pain cracked open my heart to others' suffering and showed me in no way am I unique; we are all damaged and fragile. My strangled voice helped me learn that I am not this body. I am bigger than these sounds. I am life without boundaries with a heart as big as the sky. I am Presence in a vulnerable human container.

Silence

Vickie Manz

Silence wraps softly around her warm body
No beginning, no end
A moment of perfection
Alone and complete
She snuggles under its warmth
Free from all need, only this moment, perfection.

The wife, the mother, the grandmother rests; life rests.
Silence feeds a hunger never embraced before.
Impenetrable yet soothing, feeding her soul

Her eyes close, she sighs into the moment.
Deepening the connection
Honoring the truest part of who she is.

Building a Shrine

Tracey Schmidt

My life so far
Has been like
Trying to put a very large love
Through a pinhole.
I have tried to make myself
Small enough to fit into this world.
But finally the shell has rent in two—
And the shrine of my being has emerged.

We are guided home on an invisible thread—
One day the distance between our self and the hole
Simply
Disappears.

And then the love fits perfectly.

There is so much work to do in this world
When we could simply choose
To be ecstatically happy.
To take rocks and driftwood and build an altar
To all that is good inside of us—
And to set our one shining life
On fire.

Future Plans

Ellen Beegel

I plan for the sun to rise most mornings. And sometimes rain.
I plan to stretch my body, watching through the window as
      breezes toss the maple leaves.
I plan to drink strong coffee, to eat dark toast smeared with
      peanut butter and blueberries.

I plan to accept the silence of living alone.
To be grateful for friendships.

I plan for my skin to grow thin and wrinkled.
To lie awake in bed in the morning, stiff and dream-soaked.
To watch blue and purple paint blend into a hundred watery paths.
The phone will ring, but I will not answer it.

The sun will set.
Stars will appear.
Venus and Saturn, Scorpio and Orion.

I plan to tolerate loneliness.
I plan to tolerate the departures of airplanes.
I plan to sing.
To let go.
To merge into the earth.
To become brown mulch.
To become oak.
To become.

A Well-Earned Face

Grace Ellis

Just look at the woman in the photograph. Her face is wrinkled. Her hair is white and wispy. A tooth is crooked. None of that is what you notice most. There is a glow that lights her face from within. And a sturdiness that is stronger than her frailty. A kindness. A serenity. Joy.

I remember the older women—mostly Quakers and Mennonites and Catholic nuns—at the anti-war marches in Washington, DC, in 1967-68. Their faces were calm as they stood on street corners or joined the protests, holding their signs. I said to my twenty-one-year-old self, "When I grow up, I want to have a face like that."

I don't have it yet. When I look in the mirror, I see white hair, wrinkles, collapsing cheeks, but only a hint of that peace like a river in the soul. But there's still time, I hope. Meanwhile, although I do not judge those who have made different choices, I refuse to dye my hair. I will work hard to lose a few pounds, I will floss my teeth, I will go after my post-menopausal chin whiskers with tweezers, I will put moisturizer on my face (but no make-up), and there will be no botox injections for me. Because someday—someday maybe sooner than later—I hope to have one of those well-worn, radiant faces.

I don't think anyone gets a face like that without suffering—without the sorrow that breaks us open and leaves in its wake a sensitivity to the slightest hint of another person's grief. Distress, when we are in the midst of it, does not seem to be a gift, but it is. And there's no need to go looking for sadness. If we live long enough, we are bound to have plenty of tears.

A face like this draws other people like a magnet. Here, it says, is someone you can trust. Here is someone who will understand. Here is someone who will laugh with you, cry with you, and share a gem of wisdom—but only if you ask.

Sometimes I imagine Mother Teresa (I know you've seen pictures of her face—glowing despite—or perhaps because of—her inner struggles). I imagine her on a television make-over show. "Now, Mamacita," says the plastic surgeon/make-up artist, "a little cream here, a pinch here, some color, and we can certainly do something with those lips." And in this daydream of mine, every-one—everyone in the studio audience, everyone at home—takes one look at Mother Teresa's sparkling eyes and laughs and laughs at the absurdity of retouching a face that is already exactly what it is meant to be.

Realizations

To be a writer, I had to
become self-full. This is where
the struggle lies, not in
taking another class, earning
an MFA, getting published,
being a household name,
or earning a huge advance
for a book. The struggle is
in being ourselves.

PTM

. . . .

The Well-Used Teacup

Nancy Newlin

All these uppity, priceless teacups were shouting so loud at me to get out of the china cabinet that I was sure Sarah and her parents heard the clamor. Didn't they? But the cabinet doors were locked and there was no way that I could have left, even if I had wanted to. So I sat defiantly where I was and plucked dust balls from the corners to put into my ears and muffle the noise. I sat and waited.

It was beautiful, young Sarah who put me in here with all these fancy painted cups and saucers with rims of gold and hand-painted designs, made all over the world, purchased one by one, boxed carefully and stowed in luggage for the return trip. Yes, I'd heard them talking.

"She found me in Shanghai at an antiques dealer."

"He ordered me specially made. It took a year for me to be sent here. My porcelain is from a place so remote that only the potter knows where it is. He collects this clay only once a year and stores it to age for five years before he makes anything with it. My gold is twenty-four karat from. . . ."

"Enough," I yelled. "Enough, all you snobbish teacups. You're the only ones who care about all of this. Sarah's mother and father just unpacked you and stuffed you into this cabinet. Neither one of them even knows that you're still here. When was the last time you were used?"

They all gasped at once.

"Used? What do you mean, used? We are precious. We are not to be used, only admired," they said in unison.

"You all sneer at me, but at least I'm used. What is the use of admiration?" I asked. "It hasn't gotten you out of this cabinet, has it?"

"I, on the other hand, have been used—well used. Sarah uses me for her tea parties. So I have a chip here and there, and she's washed me so often and so hard that the silver along my edge is almost gone. But I consider this all to be an honor, an honor to be used. I also get out of this dreary china cabinet for a while. And sometimes the tea party is outside on the porch."

"What does 'outside' mean?" one of the teacups asked.

"Oh, yes, I forgot that you don't know about outside," I said, continuing. "Sometimes Sarah puts me at Wendy's place and sometimes at hers. Her mother says she's too young to drink black tea, so there's herb tea in the teapot. Often there are fancy cookies on a pretty china plate. Sometimes they wear their play clothes and sometimes they dress up. I like the dress-up tea parties the best."

By now, the teacups were quiet.

"How can we get out of this china cabinet?" one of them asked.

"You can take turns scootching over to the front here by me. Sometimes, Sarah has other friends over for tea and needs more than two teacups, so you could be chosen, along with me."

At that, the teacups began another uproar, shouting and pushing each other out of the way of the middle front of the shelf, where the door latch was, to gain "next pick" advantage.

But one teacup, I noticed, was quiet and remained where it was. It had deep red cherries and vibrant green leaves painted on a bright white background with a narrow gold line around the rim of the cup and the saucer.

I left the other teacups to argue and jostle and went over to this teacup, slowly, so as not to startle it.

Finally, I sat down beside the cherry teacup. Just sat for a minute or two. Then I turned to it and said, "Cherry Teacup, why are you back here by yourself?"

"She bought me for Sarah," Cherry Teacup said, and tears began to roll down, "but all these other teacups shoved me to the back and won't let me near the front. I've heard Sarah say more than once, 'Where is the teacup with the cherries on it that Mommy bought for me?' but I'm so far back here on the shelf and it's so dark that she can't see me and her arms aren't long enough to get me out of here anyway."

"Oh my," I said, "that's very sad. You need to be up here in the front with me."

A very large teacup with a broad, deep shape and dark design on it turned around and said with a snarl, "No you don't. Another teacup has already taken that spot. Cherry Teacup will have to wait for its turn."

Considering its response, I thought that this teacup might be a bit difficult to deal with and also that Sarah would probably never choose it for her tea parties. It would be a better size for her father's hands.

So I turned around and said, "Oh, my, you are the tallest and largest teacup in the cabinet. Have you considered the possibility that you might feel out of place at a little girl's tea party?"

The teacup, which had pulled itself taller even than it was to stare down at me, sat back onto its saucer. Its belligerent look turned to one of pondering and thinking. It was silent for a while.

"Actually," said Big Teacup, "I hadn't thought of that. I just didn't want to be left out."

And then an idea came to me.

"Big Teacup, what would you think about making up some cards with numbers on them and passing one out to each teacup? And how would you like to be the manager of us all, allowing us to go to the front of the line, one by one, as one teacup is taken from the cabinet, in order by the numbers on our cards? Then, when we return, you can direct us to the back of the line to wait for our next turn."

"That's such a good idea," Big Teacup said, "that I truly wish that I'd thought of it first. But how are you going to get all the rest of the teacups to agree to this? They've already jostled for position. And also remember, you'll no longer always be chosen for the tea parties. Your turn will take many weeks or months to come up again."

Oh no, I thought, I won't be getting out of here as often as I once did. I'll have to wait for my turn, and I'll no longer be Sarah's favorite. I felt very sad when I thought about missing out on so many tea parties.

And then I remembered that, just a short time ago, I called all of the other teacups uppity and snobbish. Was I now being uppity and snobbish about my own place as Sarah's favorite teacup?

Oh my, this is embarrassing, I thought. I called them snobbish, but I'm that way, too. I guess I'll take my turn with all the others. And I don't even know any of them because I've always been at the front of the cabinet. As we stand next to each other in line, we'll all get to know each other better.

"What do you think about that idea, Cherry Teacup?" I asked.

"I like it a lot, because then all of us have equal chances to be chosen. And also I'll be included with the rest of the teacups."

"Teacup friends," I said rather loudly, "Big Teacup has come up with a great idea."

"I have?" said Big Teacup.

"Yes, you have," I said. "Big Teacup suggests that we all take numbered cards to know our place in line so that all of us will be chosen at some time for Sarah's tea party. Big Teacup has also agreed to make up all the cards and help us maintain order here on the shelf. What do you think of that?"

All the teacups rattled on their saucers and one by one said enthusiastically, "Yes!"

"It's settled then," I said. "And I do have one favor to ask."

No one said anything, so I went on.

"Sarah's mother bought Cherry Teacup especially for her daughter's tea parties, but it has been stuck way back here on the shelf since it arrived a long time ago. Can we agree to let this teacup go to the head of the line, just this once, so that it's sure to be chosen next time?"

There was a bit of silence, and then the teacups rattled on their saucers once more and said, "Yes!"

Some weeks later, Sarah invited so many of her friends over for tea that she had to take six teacups and saucers out of the cabinet. After they were returned to the shelf, one of them told us that Sarah's mother had joined the tea party and had said, "I didn't know that we had so many very lovely teacups. I'm so glad that your friends came over so that you could get these other teacups out and use them."

Over time, as all of us were used at Sarah's tea parties, life in the china cabinet became quieter and friendlier, and the china cabinet itself seemed brighter.

Effulgence

Tracey Schmidt

All winter long
I tried and tried
To find a way
Through your sloped frown
And terse eyes.

I never knew how
To please you.
Though in my
Uncomfortable heart
I yearned for your
Joy
And exclusive hand

It is lonely knowing you.

But one day
I understood
The barren judgment
You inhabit.

Nothing
Enough

No deep reservoir of
Care
In which to dip.
And so
I learned to

Love my own
Benevolent landscape
And drink
From my own
Effulgent
Cupped hands.
The inherited
Disapproving clutch
Opened—
Releasing
A radiant drop of
Freedom.

Why Not Now?

Heidi Stewart

I long for the day that I can play with abandon, just being in the moment, without the heavy feeling of being "responsible" for so many others' problems and issues.

As I play, I soak in the day. I soak in the moment, hearing the birds, soaring along with them in my mind, feeling the sun pouring down on my skin, turning it brown.

Laughing freely, with no concerns about "looking good" or acting "appropriate" or of what someone may say or think about me, just another "Wild Woman," loose on the town!

I long for the day that I can sit at a café with a friend, sipping a cool mango margarita, exposing my breast tops to whomever may see them—loose, wild, free, no concerns or cares to keep me from being that creative, fun woman who loves life, people, creating, art, writing, and doing crazy "unheard" of things, like making a scene in a restaurant just to see the people's reactions!

But also being that gentle, giving, real, loving, approachable, caring woman I really am, without pretense—without the rigid sense and walls of "Attorney," just me, woman, mother, grandmother, writer, gardener, herbalist, artist, lover, Spirit who came to this time to share her gifts with others, all of them, without reservation or hesitation. A woman who doesn't let a preconceived character creation stop her from blooming, being all of the person and Spirit that she really is and can be so that when she looks back she is saying, "I gave it my all and I have no regrets." Flowing skirts, long hair, loose, relaxed body, wild times, and a smile with a touch of craziness to it, are all I ask and long for . . . wait . . . why not now?

Sunbeam Senders

Nancy Newlin

It takes a lot of energy for me to begin again—anything. The song that didn't align with the music as melodically as I had hoped, the dress I was sewing that I stuffed into a drawer when it wasn't turning out as the pattern envelope showed, the decorating project that I lost interest in. And, what about loving a new man?

First, I'll pull out the thorns and grind off the calloused places that came from that previous relationship. I'll put salve on those hurts, treating them tenderly. I'll get my body moving in new ways. I won't go back to the places we used to go to. From the remnants of that relationship, I'll pick out, tidy up, and store away the good parts. I'll send him a card to thank him for his part in my life journey. New things learned, new places visited, new insights gained. Maybe someday I'll open the place where these memory trinkets are stored and think again about whether they can stay—or if they must go.

My greatest challenge is to nurture my broken heart—but was it really broken? Maybe it wasn't. Maybe it was a bit bruised by boredom, his lack of appreciation for me, and his stubbornness. I'll sit and drink cold tea on the back porch, mow the lawn, and tend to the safe haven of my home. I'll take down the cobwebs the spiders spun while I was out with him; make the place habitable again for myself and welcoming for a new man.

Then I'll gather in the energy that went out of me like sunbeams to be with him. He just gobbled up the sunbeams I sent and rarely sent one back. Sunbeam eaters like him are the ones you should give up first. It took me a long time to realize this. Time for that massage I've been putting off, get into the activities of the season, soak up some sunshine, take a hike, go swimming.

So, when I'm ready, filled up with new sunbeams from taking good care of myself, I'll go scouting using a new strategy—the sunbeam strategy.

I'll find, meet, and then test each new candidate for my affections by sending him a slim, bitty sunbeam of warmth to see what comes back.

If a cloud comes back, I'll move on to the next one. If a sunbeam comes back that's equal to the one I sent, that's OKAY, I'll send a bigger one. If the returned sunbeam is larger—wow!—there's a sunbeam sender who might match me. A treasure! I'll keep sending sunbeams to see what happens. Maybe just a passing fancy. Maybe love.

So many bright sunbeams of appreciation, laughter, affection, and understanding.

He sent me twofold or threefold as many
As I sent him.
He called me the sunbeam sender.
How many sunbeams
Can we send
Back and forth
Until the sun is used up?
Oh, the sun is never used up.
It's continually replenished from within by its moltenness
Like love from the heart
That increases as it receives love in return.
Neverending.

Buster Brown

Jeannette Reid

The shoe store where I sit slouched and swing my dangling feet.
The outside window showed the hip new styles—penny loafers,
saddle shoes in brown, dark blue, maroon.

I know my fate—the sturdy oxford.

First the metal measuring device—cold through my sock and
steely.

"Stand up. Stand straight. Put all your weight," the little mus-
tached man instructs. His stubby fingers push against my socks.
Off he scurries through a door, returns, removes the top from each
cardboard box (they teach this in shoe-selling school), lifts out
his plum, a shiny shoe exactly like the scuffed ones I am wearing.
"A whole half-inch longer," he announces to my mother with his
pursed-lipped smile.

He lifts my heel, rams in my foot, pulls the laces super tight
and knots the bow, then says it's time to walk the bridge—stupid
affair that curves up to a rise where he and mother squeeze the feet
and talk about my instep. Next the famed X-ray machine. I stand,
each foot shoved in a slot, and look down through weird binoculars
to see the bony insides of my foot.

Outside the store, I step ahead five feet or more. Flat refuse to
hold the bag that holds my ugly shoes.

Breakdown

Ginger Graziano

I have a Polaroid taken of Jenny, Jeremy, and me in 1977 after I left Vinny, and we moved to Irvington, New Jersey, after we came back from our cross-country camping trip. The three of us squeezed up so close to the camera that we look distorted. I study their red cheeks, their open expectant faces. Was this after the hospital, after I spun out of control? Their faces look wary, as if they were thinking, *Can we trust you to be solid? Can we trust that you will not fall away again?*

I look like I had screwed up my courage, and we recorded the moment to prove it.

I had wanted to leave them with Vinny because I didn't think I could raise them. I felt shaky and scared, maybe I couldn't rise to this. I remember Jenny coming down the hallway of our house in South Orange after Vinny told her I was leaving. She stood in front of me and demanded, "Take me with you." She was six. I said yes. I didn't know how I would do it, only that I would.

After I left with the children, my life broke down. I could no longer keep up the cheery momentum or fantasy that everything would be okay in three months or that Vinny was the only problem.

I fell off the cliff of all the safety my parents had taught me, the false safety of not facing my emotions. They rose up ugly and demanding, and I couldn't stuff them back in. My former life cracked like dried mud and crumbled off me until I was naked and raw, unable to play the game, unable to do anything but hallucinate and shake in fear. I shook down the foundation of the rotted house I stood in, shook with all my might until I hit the ground and it was solid. But I didn't see it then. I only saw that I was crazy. I'd let all my demons out to parade before me and everyone else. Ashamed, I couldn't hold in all the emotions that my family had taught me were unacceptable.

What I didn't know then was that what I did saved me, but the locked ward of a mental hospital didn't feel like a breakthrough. It felt like I was sliding down a long dark passageway towards madness and at the bottom was a door. If I opened it, death beckoned, that blessed relief of letting it all go and jumping into oblivion.

I thought of all the years between then and now. How my children saved me, how I drew pictures of them in the hospital, knowing that somehow I was going to have to pull myself together enough to walk out, go home, and raise them. I loved them dearly. They held for me the love I couldn't hold for myself. In their innocent open faces, I saw that there might be hope, there might be a way out and it was by loving them more than I could love myself. I took their hands and let them lead me back into life. And, they so willingly took my hands that I was humbled and made right enough to pull myself out of hell.

Circling the Shadows

*...our shadow side hides, not
some terrible depravity, but our
unidentified and unrealized
potential. Once recognized and
refined, the darkness reveals itself
as 90 percent gold...the deeper
the writer is willing to go within
herself, the more profound will be
the effect on her words.*

PTM

. . . .

Harvest

Kathy Sievert

Like drunken revelers
coyotes celebrate the bounty of the season,
gorging on fallen apples,
prancing and pouncing in the frosty moonlight,
yipping and yowling in frenzied chorus,
a rowdy midnight serenade.

Inside the darkened house,
alone and alert, an old woman listens,
recalls another October eve, long gone:
a girl, flushed and feverish,
offers her lover an apple, ripe as sin,
laughs as he bites into juicy flesh,
tastes the sweetness on his tongue,
savoring this ritual of seduction.

Lulled by coyotes singing,
cradled in memory's embrace,
she softens into sleep,
inhaling the essence of apples
and smiling.

Burt

Cindy Peterson

I grew alarmed, he held me so tight, this skinny rail of a man. There was much more than a hug goodbye—there was a clinging to life, a sense of,

"Oh God, won't you stay!"

The old eyes watered behind the wire rims of his thick glasses. I began to realize that stepping into Burt's life was a commitment, for my presence had burst the dam of loneliness.

I seem to gravitate towards the elderly, especially since my journey with Mother. Steeling myself to walk through those glass doors, down those squeaky clean hallways, glimpsing skeletons of frail and failing flesh entrapping souls longing to be free. I loved them, every one. The crazy hunched woman clinging to her doll, the white haired Doc in a captain's hat whizzing down the halls with his flagpole fixed to his wheel chair. Around the corner to my owl-eyed mother gazing transfixed out her sliding glass doors,

"Oh honey! I'm so glad you're here. Look! Look!" She beckoned for me to follow the line of her gaze.

"There's a little boy trapped in the top of that crane! He was bad and his father locked him there in that little box."

Looking across the street, I saw a gigantic construction crane piercing the sky. High aloft the operator sat in the little cubicle.

"Mother," I cooed, "That's the man who runs the crane. It's okay—no worries."

She penetrates my eyes through her wide round glasses. For an extraordinary space in time we gaze at one another. I see the wheels of her reason sorting through what I have said. Confusion jumbles any cohesive train of thought. She turns back to the glass.

"Look! Look! There's a little boy in the top of that crane! He was bad and his father locked him up there in that little box!"

I close the drapes.

Burt's mind is clear, analytical, ordered, precise. I drop in and he begins to explain something to me. Like the way in which he has engineered his blackberry trellis. Without missing a beat, he moves into an explanation of how moisture is provided his berries by the natural stream above his lot and how he has meticulously built a stream bed that manages flood water in winter. Then I am given an ordered accurate timeline of the stream's history, whose properties it runs through, the conflicts between which neighbors it has caused over the fifty years he has lived here.

Reams of information stored in his memory pour forth. I am amazed, speechless, so many accurate, perfectly ordered facts coming from the mind of this white haired, eighty-eight-year-old retired engineer. Not just facts, but stories, impressions, opinions. Despite my amazement, I am fighting heavy eyelids mesmerized by the drone of the nonstop recitation. I keep eye contact as I nod my head trying to stay engaged, interested. I'm losing the battle in the warm room. Then he stops abruptly.

"I'm sorry. I know I talk too much." We both take a big sigh and then off he goes again. I love the man. So starved for someone to listen to his story, to the beauty of his memory, his history. I feel like the last one left to bear witness. Like he is piling volumes and volumes of rare and last-print books in my arms. How can I hold them all? It is in the reaching my hand to eagerly take each volume, one by one with gratefulness that matters. He is reviewing his life and he is grieving its end.

Having all I can hold for one day, I apologize that I must be getting along. We walk to the car and I get the hug. That bone-crushing hug that brings me back. That hug that reminds me that I have made a commitment, and I must not forget.

As I drive away up the narrow woodsy driveway, I glance in my rearview mirror to see him pressing his hanky under his glasses to wipe the tears away.

Took Out the Tattered

Robin Russell Gaiser

"We have seven hospice patients," she said, quickly jotting down their names and room numbers to the best of her memory on a torn out, wrinkled notebook page, then handing it to me. The same odor, the one that mixes floor cleaner with old person skin and clothing scents, bodily functions, and starchy cafeteria smells of macaroni and cheese dinners, welcomed me as soon as I entered the hall.

Seven hospice patients. Shall I go to the ones I know? Or start my routine with a newcomer to this exclusive club of the dying. I fasten my Certified Music Practitioner badge to my sweater, grab my guitar and harp, and find the first room.

I am disturbed by the apparent age of my first patient. A stroke victim, maybe fifty-five. Perfect skin and beauty hidden way back now in her hollow blue eyes. I begin our session, guitar slow and easy with my voice. "Peace is flowing like a river, flowing out of you and me." She is restless and struggles to move. "Flowing out into the desert, setting all the captives free." I sense her damaged body trying to get out of itself. Out of the entrapment. Her eyes open and close. Is she looking for me?

I know she hears me. I just know it.

I change tunes. This time I only sing—no guitar. She'll get these words. "Almost heaven, West Virginia, Blue Ridge Mountains, Shenandoah River." Do I see her recognize? Is she thinking of her home, now far away, as the song says? Or is she thinking of heaven, the home where she's going? Or is she thinking at all?

I see a droplet of moisture in her eye; her head turns toward me now. The droplet falls to the pillow. The melody, I know, reaches her. Perhaps it's enough to convey to her, to me, that she's still alive somewhere. Her arm reaches up, as so many do when heaven is so near, but it begins to quiver. Then settles back down. I hope the music is helping her relax. Her breathing is easy and steady, so heaven is farther away than she thinks. "Almost heaven," as the song says.

I sing another song, a blessing. Low-key, mellow alto—the best for calming. She is more restful now. Her eyes close. Her chest rises and falls. I pray. That's all I can do besides sing. I leave her, harp and guitar in hand, and move on to the next patient.

But I cannot help but take a little of her with me.

Flash

Maggie Wynne

There is no time for evening in this place they say.
She'll find no slant, no amber light among the bound, the elderly.
Click, the darkest darkness falls. Flash they make it day.

Songs are sung, time announced for games she cannot play.
She eats among the clanging trays, food she cannot see.
There is no time for evening in this place they say.

Crowded, alone, she finds no space to dream, to hope, to pray.
She longs to watch the evening come. They will not let her be.
Click, the darkest darkness falls. Flash they make it day.

She used to wait for him, for love, for hours to while away.
But now he's gone and she remains with these who cannot flee.
There is no time for evening here they say.

Time to bathe, they lift her, twist her another way.
"Now's the time to clean you up" life moves at their decree.
Click the darkest darkness falls. Flash they make it day.

But silence speaks a final word, they will not have their way.
They cannot schedule this. She'll go where she can see
A place with time for evening, each slant, each amber ray.
When darkest darkness falls, flash it will be day.

Dementia

Betsy Fletcher

I sit
And rock

I wait

I see the schoolmarm
Starched shirt
Bun tight
Facing
The Blackboard

Erasing
Is
Mrs. Witt's
Vocation

She erases
The first letter of my name
Then
The next
Slowly
In
Circles
One
Continuous movement

She never stops
Never turns
She is busy

Erasing
Erasing
Every speck

Soon, very soon,
The time comes
For the sponge
To wash away
The remaining dust
Everything
Wet blackness

Then
What remains
Appears
Dried and blank

She is fastidious
Insidious

I wait

I watch

Seeing

I sit
And rock

Facing
The Blackboard

Longing

Deborah Cantrell

Longing—well, that one is easy—seven years clean, and every day I fantasize about my death cocktail—when I can have all I want of the Big H one more time, and I can soar again on the orgasmic mix we took on our jet to Thailand. We were so high in customs that when they detained Hubertos, I thought it was funny. I couldn't remember our lawyer's name, much less his freaking phone number. My speed dial didn't work in security anyway.

They searched his bags and found some mild stuff, just the weed and pills. They didn't get my needles and powder because they were zipped and locked in the hidden pocket of my Louie V, and I wouldn't open it for them. "Kiss my bony ass!" I screamed. "Touch me, and it's rape!" They let me go to the hotel, and Hubertos went to jail. I thought it was funny.

I called Hubertos' brother in Palm Beach. "I'll have the Miami law firm handle this one. They have offices in Bangkok," he snarled at me. I thought that was funny too.

We were trying to get to Vietnam because the best and purest drugs were there—fresh from the fields. I forget what we were celebrating. Maybe I had won over the fences in Rome at the World Equestrian Games. I won often then. We were always celebrating something.

Tiny, shimmering crystals sparkling on the glass, the finest powder, each molecule smiling at me—a snort before I shoot. Crashing in Thailand was not my plan. The lawyers sprung Hubertos from jail, so I told our pilot to take us to Guam. I don't know why I said, "Guam." I don't remember if we ever went there or what we did or how long we flew. I just know somehow the damn pilot put us down on a private strip just north of LAX. He dumped our good stuff out the window on the tarmac and told me I was so high

I could have flown home without the plane. He quit.

Then there was the white time: glossy white surfaces, stainless steel, metallic sounds, antiseptic smells, fluorescent lights, the hospital, my doctors, again, and all over. The ambulance ride to rehab, the days of shakes and pukes, the awful dreams, the other stinking idiots, new shrinks, different meds, and after months that my mind thought were years, I left clean. Eighty-nine pounds, ulcers, twitches, chain-smoking Camels, sucking on peppermint candies—no more show jumping for me. I sold the jumpers. I bought a sable and a diamond bracelet. I ride an old, Andalusian stallion now—dressage—around and around the oblong ring going from one letter to the next. Longing . . . longing . . . longing.

I was meant to fly, to soar. Taking the high fences on a gifted thoroughbred, with hundreds cheering from the stands, that was a thrill, an adrenaline rush, but it was never enough. The brief instant of freedom as we sailed over the jump, turning in mid-air to look for the next one, it passed too fast; it was over before it began. I wanted it to last longer, much longer. I had to ride a bigger rocket, break the sound barrier, shoot into the sky, and never look back.

I did. I found a way. And I paid. Turns out it was not funny at all. But, today, seven years clean, I know precisely what was in that last dream cocktail mix on the way to Thailand, and I'll have it again before I die. I promise I will. One last ride—one last high fence—the longing will be over.

Sloan Kettering

Ginger Graziano

Sloan Kettering sits at the lower edge of hospital row, a few blocks from Hunter College and some of my happiest years. I gazed at the 59th Street Bridge from the eighth floor window of the pediatric oncology ward. Small, bald children walked the floor with plasma drips or blood bags attached into their veins. Like kids, they stood on the metal wheels of the structure that held the bags and rolled through the halls. Some simply lay in bed.

Parents were always around. In the communal kitchen's refrigerator, we placed labeled containers with our children's foods and treats. The nurses' station was nearby and all night its lights shone as we got up to tend to our children. I met other mothers washing dishes or doing laundry late at night and we shared our stories and traded advice. This family of mothers, thrown together by our children's cancer, was a comfort. I met mothers from the Middle East, from expensive suburban towns in Connecticut, from neighborhoods in the Bronx and Queens; black, Hispanic, white, rich or poor, all of us praying and making bargains with our various gods—Allah, Jesus, Yahweh. We slept in reclining chairs or propped up on two chairs, a nightmarish rest where morning felt like a hangover. We stared down at people walking to work, delivery trucks with handcarts, or taxis with their red lights in a row funneling workers southward. We watched a picture of a world we vaguely remembered. And, as we glanced away, our children lay, bald-headed and pale on white sheets with saline drips and needles in their veins; bedpans, water pitchers, and curtains that gave illusory privacy from the family on the other side who was mirroring our early morning.

I could hear the roar of the city beneath me, rising up from the street. Horns honked and planes grazed the low clouds. I got up exhausted and refilled Jeremy's glass with fresh water, greeted the nurse, gentle, loving angel who worked there among the children.

There was caring and love but the news was harsh. We were where there was no going back. We had examined this alley—this eddy in the stream of life—for a door out but found none. His platelets were at twenty-five, dangerously low. No more rounds of chemo were planned; no more poison in hopes of killing the killer inside Jeremy before it killed him. His body was strong, but the cancer was stronger. The delicate balance had been tipped. I fingered my beads calling on God's various names, looking for hope. There was none. It was the last thing to die before the reality of death took hold.

Dawn's red glow streaked over Manhattan, and I stood there loving my son, tending to his needs. He didn't want to be a burden. We still believed in miracles.

Two Kinds of Deliverance

Jennifer Lynn Browning

There are always two kinds of deliverance—that which saves us
and that which destroys us. We are each of us destined to make the
choice between staying and going, between living with the pain or
giving up from despair. We must decide for ourselves which choice
we will make, which of Frost's paths we will trod. Yet, in that moment of deliverance, we find poised, like an iridescent drop of mo-
tor oil, our life's path, our life's choices; this final choice decides us
and sets us free regardless of which side we choose.

As she labored through each breath and tried to force air between the pockets of mucus in her throat and mouth, I know she
had a question of which choice she would make. She could choose
to be the valiant soldier and carry on despite the pain, the embar-
rassment, the sheer absurdity of her disease. Her other choice, the
one which must have seemed so much more appealing, though in
some ways so much harder, was of course to finally lay down arms
and concede defeat.

Leaning over her that bright, blistering fall day, I saw her make
her choice. It wasn't a focus of the eyes; that focus was five days
gone. It wasn't an expression; for, that too the morphine had stolen.
It wasn't even a change in position. Yet, though it wasn't visible, I
still saw the moment the decision was made. A voice crossed the
threshold in greeting and now with us all gathered around her, she
made her choice.

A Rising Wind

Anonymous

In a rising wind
The white sails fill
And take my sad, sad thoughts
Out to sea.

After Words

Acknowledgment

Stephanie Hawkins

I previously thought that writing to a prompt was a writing process that one surrenders to in order to get to the "real writing process." Now I understand that this process *is* the real writing process. That one can write fiction, non-fiction, short stories, etc. through prompts … confirms what I have always known as the true connection to divine knowing …. The writing is not coming from me but through me, if I can just keep myself out of the way long enough.

NOTES ON CONTRIBUTORS

Ellen Beegel – Ellen used to roam the earth as a nomad, raised twins as a single parent, and began taking ClarityWorks classes when she moved to Asheville, North Carolina, in 2007. She lives with a feisty cat companion, sings with a joyful women's chorus, and loves the way dark clouds gather before a storm. Writing reminds her who she is.

Suzanne Blievernicht – Suzanne, a native of Atlanta, Georgia, and mother of two daughters, lived in Richmond, Virginia; Heidelberg, Germany; and Greensboro, North Carolina, before settling on a farm in Fletcher, North Carolina. Peggy Millin and her classes and retreats have inspired and energized her to creatively explore and distill her life's experiences on paper. An RN for forty-eight years, she is a medical practice coordinator and experiences the joy of professionally collaborating with her husband.

Kathleen Rada Boswell – Kathleen has attended and joyously written at both the Lake Logan and Seabrook Retreats since 2009. She is a nomad who resides in Texas, Tennessee, and Indiana. Kathleen also enjoys canning food, cooking, and painting. She has taken pride in being a daughter, sister, wife, mother, and grandmother, but will love finally saying, "published writer."

Jennifer Browning – Jennifer is a native of Asheville, North Carolina, who teaches composition and literature at a local community college. She is a collector and creator of stories through writing, scrapbooking, and photography. She has participated in several ClarityWorks classes and retreats.

Deborah Cantrell – Deborah was born in Tennessee, reared in Arkansas, educated in Mississippi, and now lives in Texas. She enjoys travel, history, and horses. Thanks to ClarityWorks creative writing retreats, she learned the joy of "writing in circles" and now aspires to be a writer for the rest of her life.

Kimberly Childs – Kimberly has always enjoyed writing—her father wrote for the *New York Daily Mirror*, so it's in her blood. When she lost her voice in 1997, however, writing became a necessity. She moved to Asheville, North Carolina, in 2000 and discovered Peggy Millin's ClarityWorks soon after. The women's writing group became a lifeline of self-expression. Writing was a path of healing and connection to community. She found that her writes were coalescing into autobiography that is now—all these years later—finished. She gives much gratitude to Peggy for the support of ClarityWorks.

Joanne Costantino – Joanne, born and raised in Philadelphia and now residing in South Jersey, has been retreating with Peggy's ClarityWorks since 2007 at both Lake Logan and Seabrook. Her first ClarityWorks retreat came on the heels of a steady stream of returning grown children and their children, while attempting to complete her college degree and finishing treatment for breast cancer. She needed a break from that routine and through the retreats found all that life experience provides the guts of her writing. Her writing is about real events and people who couldn't be made up if she tried. The payoff is apparent to her husband, Mike; he gifts the retreat as a Christmas present! The inaugural publication of *Tall Tales and Short Stories from South Jersey,* an anthology published by the South Jersey Writers group, opens with Joanne's story, "The Philly Girl" in Jersey. With that she became "actually published." You can follow Joanne's blog at *www.weneedmoresundaydinners.blogspot.com*

Beth Dewan – Beth began writing as a vehicle for healing and awakening. She has attended both Seabrook and Lake Logan retreats where she found loving support within the circle of writers. Beth writes to uncover her soul. She currently spends time in the quiet solitude of nature where she can hear her soul-song and feel her heartbeat with joy. A nurse by training, she now runs the Dragonfly Inn, a B&B in Culebra, Puerto Rico *http://www.dragonflyinnculebra.com*

Joy Wallace Dickinson – Joy grew up in Orlando, Florida, where she rushed on Saturdays to buy the latest Nancy Drew mystery with her weekly allowance. She writes a feature in the *Orlando Sentinel* about aspects of Central Florida's past and is also the author of *Orlando: City of Dreams.* Joy is grateful to Peggy Tabor Millin and the sisters of Peggy's writing circles for their wisdom, generosity, courage, and support.

Cheryl Dietrich – Cheryl retired as an Air Force officer in 2000. Two years later she moved to Asheville and started Peggy Tabor Millin's writing classes. This was a lifesaver for her. She has since written a memoir, *In Formation,* about her years in the Air Force, to be published by Yucca Press. In 2014, she was diagnosed with ALS and died in January 2015 at the age of 65. Her writing sisters will miss her perceptive wit and the clarity and depth of her prose.

Grace Ellis – Grace spent twenty years teaching English, mostly in North Carolina community colleges. She has written textbooks, poems, and articles, but she most enjoys writing for the stage. She has been fortunate to see about twenty-five of her plays performed in churches and schools and the Greensboro Cultural Arts Center. Her experiences at Peggy Millin's Lake Logan retreats developed her ability to imagine the sound of her own voice speaking the words as she writes them. She and a friend continue to meet and write to Peggy's prompts, and the result of one of these sessions recently was selected for the *Winston-Salem Writers Anthology.*

Lucia Ellis – Lucia believes in miracles and magic, in wonder and whimsy. She lives a marvelous life in Atlanta, Georgia, where she thinks about writing more than she writes. She makes art on Tuesdays, is a psychotherapist most days, and, every day, she is in love with the most miraculous, magical, wonder-filled and whimsical partner. She is grateful for every opportunity to write with a group and has found Peggy's Seabrook and Lake Logan weeks to be life changing. Her gratitude and admiration abound for all the women she has ever shared a prompt with.

Ginny Martin Fleming – Ginny first met Peggy at a North Carolina Writers' Network Spring Conference in 2005. In fact, she can be heard reading a prompt writing she wrote during the workshop using the verb "swim" on Peggy's CD *Family Matters: The Power of the Personal Story*. Ginny has written since childhood as a way to discover herself and to make sense of her world, often surprised at the revelations. She has lived in both North Carolina and Arkansas, and now splits her time between her home in Wake Forest and her little beach house at Holden Beach, North Carolina, her favorite place in the world. She loves writing, yoga, and beachcombing almost as much as being a mother and grandmother. *www.ginnymartinfleming.com*

Betsy Fletcher – Betsy started writing poetry when she was 11 years old at summer camp in North Carolina. After living in Colorado and Washington State for many years, she returned to become a full time North Carolina resident in 2009. Betwixt and between, she seriously put pen to paper again through ClarityWorks retreats and classes. Her first prompt was "broom." Now that the cobwebs have been swept out, a maturing poet has emerged. She looks out the window a lot. Betsy makes her home in Pisgah Forest, North Carolina, partly because the name of the community is more poetic than nearby Brevard.

Mary Freen – Mary loves playing with words and fabric, though not usually at the same time. She seldom indulged her love of writing until she discovered Fearless Writing on the Blue Ridge, Lake Logan, 2011. "This writing retreat was a gift to myself, and writing in circle," she says, "was like opening a door. When you keep the pen moving, you don't even know what your soul has to say until you read the words back to yourself." Now retired, she writes to explore her love of the natural world, animals (wild and not so), and family (mostly not so).

Robin Russell Gaiser – Robin has lived up and down the east coast but now joyfully finds her home in the Blue Ridge Mountains of Asheville, North Carolina, where she wandered into Peggy's writing classes. "I found my voice after three sessions in Peggy's writing room and haven't looked back." Four published stories and an upcoming book, *Musical Morphine*, about her work as a therapeutic musician, a new website, a couple of Appalachian dulcimer students, a little storytelling, a lot of swimming, kayaking, walking. Add travel to see the kids and grandkids, plus trips out west and to her ancestral home in the Adirondack Mountains of upstate New York. Second book already envisioned. *www.robingaiser.com*

Ginger Graziano – Ginger moved from New York City to Asheville, North Carolina, in 2001. She tells by the size of the trees she's planted how long since she traded buildings for mountains. She creates graphic design for regional and national clients, sculpts clay figures that tell her their stories. Her grandson shows her the magic. The birds she feeds sing of freedom, joy, and adventure. All gifts. In October she flew to Ecuador to see what the sky looked like from the Southern Hemisphere. She discovered Peggy Millin's classes shortly after arriving in Asheville and her writing changed as a result of writing in community. A chapter from her soon-to-be-published memoir, *See, There He Is*, has been published in Ball State University's online magazine, *Embodied Effigies*. *www.gingergraziano.com*

Stephanie Hawkins – Stephanie has attended Peggy Millin's writing workshops for the past two years. Writing in a supportive circle of women nourishes the soul and allows her to reclaim her artist self. She has been a dancer, healer, photographer, and writer for many years but only reclaimed this part of her self and gained the courage to share her artist voice with the world after attending Peggy's workshops. Trained in psychology and dance/movement therapy, she incorporates messages of universal consciousness in all of her work. She is the co-author of *69 Volume I: Unveiling*, a poetic and visual exploration of the intimate connection between spirituality and sensuality. She enjoys the literary genres of poetry and creative non-fiction while also serving as an academic dean at Strayer University in Douglasville, Georgia.

Sue Larmon – Sue Larmon is a former Yankee who now calls Asheville, North Carolina, her home. She teaches French at Western Carolina University in Cullowhee, and her poem emanates from a 2007 Lake Logan retreat with Peggy. She has self-published several memoirs, a children's book, and two trilogies of novels. She credits Peggy with fanning the spark of her now ongoing interest in writing.

Candy Maier – Candy Maier's laughter matched the size of her heart. She attended two Lake Logan retreats and decided to become a humorist in November 2005. Fact is, she already was. That same month, Candy passed away. The brass plaque placed at Lake Logan by her writing sisters is up on Cemetery Hill. Lucille is nearby with the best view imaginable. The plaque reads:

Candy Maier
Lover of life, laugher and Lake Logan
1952-2005

Vickie Manz – Vickie began journal writing over forty years ago as a way of self-discovery and healing. In her wildest imaginings, she dreamed of becoming a writer. After completing a successful career in real estate development and raising her family, she is at long last carving out a space for her passion—writing.

Vickie has attended several of Peggy's writing retreats where she has been encouraged to speak her truth and where she is inspired by the depth and beauty of other women openly expressing their own passion. She divides her time between Bonita Springs, Florida, and Waynesville, North Carolina. She and her husband have two grown sons and two young granddaughters.

Martha McMullen – a founding member of The Candy Fund, a scholarship set up in memory of Candy Maier for women writers in Western North Carolina, came back to writing through Peggy Millin's ClarityWorks classes. Martha's book, *Woodie on the Homefront*, was published in fall 2012.

Peggy Tabor Millin – Peggy is a child of the Colorado Desert, embracing its silence, emptiness, and power. During the last fifteen years, her ClarityWorks' writing circles have provided a safe place for women to speak their truth, stand in their power, and inspire positive change in their worlds. She is the author of *Women, Writing, and Soul-Making: Creativity and the Sacred Feminine* and *Mary's Way: Cultivating a Peaceful Heart in Trying Times*. She currently lives in Asheville, North Carolina, but will soon move to Durham. *www.clarityworksonline.com*

Nancy Newlin – Nancy spent most of her working life writing—hardware and software technical manuals. She's also the self-published author of a now out-of-print book about a historic building in her previous home town, San Jose, California. After her move to Arden, North Carolina, she dived into nonfiction writing of a different type in ClarityWorks classes and retreats as well as through classes in the Great Smokies Writing Program. Her favorite contribution to this collection is "The Well-Used Teacup" which she hopes can someday become a children's book.

Cindy Peterson – Mother, grandmother, wife and friend, Cindy is a lifetime native of the Pacific Northwest. In the fall of 2011, she joined the Fearless Women in the Blue Ridge Mountains of North Carolina. It was transforming, inspiring, and so very rich with the warmth, wit and encouragement of her Circle Writing sisters. An unforgettable experience. A lover of the beauty and wonder of creation and the One who made it, she is captivated by the journey of the soul and spirit. Her hope is to explore the depths of this gift called life through story. Many seeds were sown in her writer's soul on the shores of Lake Logan.

Alicia Porterfield – Rooted in Georgia's red clay, Alicia came to a ClarityWorks workshop in Durham in 2010, immediately signed up for Seabrook 2011 and then Lake Logan 2013. Only wild horses—and her roles as the mom of three young boys and a freelance minister—could have kept her away from the soul-shaping retreats in between. She lives in Wilmington, North Carolina, and loves to write, sing, laugh, and listen to stories in all forms.

Jeanette Reid – Jeanette retired from teaching English in Maryland and moved to Asheville in the mid-nineties. Her writing life was ignited and encouraged by Peggy Millin's "Tell It Like it Is" classes and short-story group. Love of language and playing with words led to poetry and for the last ten years she has found much joy in reading and writing poems. "It's the place where the outer world and my own inner world seem to best connect, and every day, every poem becomes an adventure of exploration."

Tracey Schmidt – At the age of nineteen, Tracey moved to Japan to live in a Buddhist monastery. The fruit of that interest is her first book of poetry, *I Have Fallen in Love with the World*, (2011, Turtle Dove Publications), as well as her multi-media touring exhibit: *The Awakening of Turtle Island: Portraits of Native Americans*. This exhibit opened for the Olympics in 1996 and has toured eighteen museums in the Southeast, including the Cherokee Museum of the American Indian. Tracey performs her poetry by memory and with music. Her first poetry/music CD, "Returning Home," features the poetry of Rumi, Hafiz, Yeats, and her own work. She teaches creativity, poetry, and photography around the country and in her hometown of Asheville, North Carolina. *www.traceyschmidt. com*. She loved Peggy's classes.

Kathy Sievert – After nineteen years away from her heart's true home, Kathy recently moved back to Alaska. She enjoys rediscovering why she feels so connected to the Great Land through hiking, photography, writing, and spending time with her young granddaughters, Ruby and Rosie. She loves to travel and explore new places, but now she knows where she belongs.

Amy Slothower – Amy, of Denver, Colorado, attended the Lake Logan retreat on a whim in 2012 after quitting her job and conducting a cursory Internet search for a writing retreat. A lifelong dabbler, she was looking for a way to renew her writing commitment and was thrilled with both the community and the techniques she found through ClarityWorks. She works as a consultant in the nonprofit industry and continues to write during the precious moments when her young son sleeps and she can stay awake.

Kimberly Smith – Kimberly is a computer systems administrator, part-time webmaster, healer, Reiki teacher, weaver, and budding herbalist. Her writing tends toward the metaphysical but may include herbal or weaving references for grounding. She infrequently blogs on *evolutionaryurge.wordpress.com* and busily keeps up the content on *perspectivesholistic.com*, which presents the varied healing work which she and her wife offer in Virginia Beach, Virginia.

Heidi Stewart – Heidi grew up traveling all over the world, but loved to come "home" to her grandmother's house in the mountains of Western North Carolina. She roamed those mountains with her brothers, and they would often find caves with arrowheads and other evidence of former habitants. She attended the first workshop Peggy Millin presented at the Asheville YWCA over fifteen years ago and several classes and retreats. She credits Peggy's classes with helping her to find her "true" voice through her writing. An attorney, Heidi recently moved from North Carolina to Portland, Oregon, where she is enjoying the beautiful natural habitat, writing, and family.

Jennifer Wheeling – Jennifer grew up on a cattle ranch in the southwest corner of Colorado. After graduating from Colorado State University with a degree in interior design and construction management, she married Joe Wheeling. Having just celebrated twenty-eight years together, traveled the world, and been self-taught organic farmers for the last seventeen years while raising two daughters, she needed something new to do with her life. She took her first leap of faith in writing in 2008 having found ClarityWorks after a google search for "women's writing retreats." One of the hardest things to learn was to be fearless in what she had to say during the writing circles. Peggy surrounded her with women who were thoughtful, empathetic, and courageous in their motivations for writing. Trying to balance the responsibilities of a large family agricultural enterprise with the personal thrill that she gets from writing has become harder and harder. Writing is beginning to win the tug-of-war as she and her husband enter a new phase of life.

Maggie Wynne – Over the many years of her participation in ClarityWorks' classes and retreats, Maggie provided a warm and loving presence to participants who attended classes and retreats in her home. She worked diligently on a young adult novel based on her grandmother's life and published *Homeward* in 2013. She also honed her skills as a poet, publishing *A Little Bit of Yesterday*, a chapbook, as well as individual poems in literary journals. She, her husband, and their two dogs live in North Carolina, dividing their time among Raleigh, Montreat, and Wrightsville Beach.

With gratitude to:

Peggy Tabor Millin, our teacher, mentor, and friend who taught us all to write fearlessly

Lake Logan Episcopal Center and St. Christopher's Camp and Conference Center for providing the settings for so much inspiration over the years

Maggie and Bob Wynne for opening their beautiful home in Montreat, NC, for ClarityWorks retreats

F. A. O'Daniel Foundation for gifting a grant which allowed the co-editors to come together for three days at Lake Logan to begin organizing *Writing in Circles*

Ginger Graziano, the graphic artist who helped to bring the book to life

Kathy Sievert, who took the time to be our "outside" reader

All the fearless writers around the world who are a part of the larger circle

Our families for their love and support during the months we devoted our time to the editing and promotion of *Writing in Circles*

CPSIA information can be obtained at www.ICGtesting.com
Printed in the USA
BVOW04s1446090415

395395BV00003B/7/P

9 780990 689102